Darcy's Unwanted Bride

By Zoe Burton

Darcy's Unwanted Bride

Zoe Burton

Published by Zoe Burton

© 2021 Zoe Burton

Early drafts of this story were written and posted on fan fiction forums in March 2021.

ISBN: 978-1-953138-09-5

Acknowledgements

First, I thank Jesus Christ, my Savior and Guide, without whom this story would not have been told. You are my Rock and my Redeemer, and I love you!

As always, I must thank my friends, Rose and Leenie. They are my sisters-in-heart and I'd be lost without them.

Thank you to each of my Patrons at Patreon, as well. There are nineteen of you now, and your support means more to me than I can say.

Table of Contents

Chapter 1 7

Chapter 2 19

Chapter 3 31

Chapter 4 45

Chapter 5 59

Chapter 6 69

Chapter 7 83

Chapter 8 97

Chapter 9 109

Chapter 10 123

Chapter 11 135

Chapter 12 149

Chapter 13 163

Chapter 14 175

Chapter 15 187

Chapter 16 197

Chapter 17 211

Chapter 18 225

Chapter 19 237

Chapter 20 251

Chapter 21 265

Chapter 22 281

Chapter 23 295

Chapter 24 307
Epilogue 319
Before you go … 329
About the Author 330
Connect with Zoe Burton 331
More by Zoe Burton 333

Chapter 1

Fitzwilliam Darcy stood rigidly at the altar of the church, his mien stoic and resolved. Beside him stood his bride, a young lady he had only met the day before. He glanced at her as he listened to the rector begin the service.

Elizabeth Bennet's cheeks were red. Indeed, her entire face was brightly burning. Like Darcy, her posture was stiff. Her jaw clenched; he could hear her teeth grind together periodically.

"Wilt thou, Fitzwilliam George Darcy, have this woman to thy wedded wife, to live together after God's ordinance in the holy estate of Matrimony? Wilt thou love her, comfort her, honor, and keep her, in sickness and in health; and, forsaking all other, keep thee only unto her, so long as ye both shall live?"

Darcy's attention snapped back to the rector. He swallowed. He could feel his father's gaze drilling into his back. He closed his eyes. "I will." His eyes opened once more and he focused them on the wall behind the clergyman.

Mr. Pound nodded and turned to Elizabeth. "Wilt thou, Elizabeth Rose Bennet, have this man to thy wedded husband, to live together after God's ordinance in the holy estate of Matrimony? Wilt thou obey him, and serve him, love, honor, and keep him, in sickness and in health; and, forsaking all other, keep thee only unto him, so long as ye both shall live?"

For a long moment, there was only silence from Elizabeth. Darcy heard Mr. Bennet's throat clear behind them and he turned his head to look at her.

"I will." Elizabeth's voice was clipped and full of defiance. Darcy could see angry tears forming in her eyes.

A few moments later, Darcy was called upon to take Elizabeth's right hand with his. Through his gloves and hers, he felt a jolt travel up his arm. He gasped at the same moment she did. Their eyes met and locked. They remained that way until his attention was called to the ring, which his father, serving in the office of best man, carried.

Darcy and his bride stood side by side through the remaining prayers and sermon. They retained the feelings of anger, resentment, and resolve that had carried them through the first part of the ceremony. Now that they were not touching, the spark that had struck them was nearly forgotten.

At the end of the ceremony, after they had signed the register, Darcy offered his arm to Elizabeth. Struck again by the shock of feeling when she curled her hand around his elbow, he remained mute as they strode down the church aisle and out the door. He escorted his new wife through the small crowd of well-wishers, handing her into the open carriage and seating himself beside her. The driver slapped the reins, putting them into motion. The trip to Longbourn was short – no more than five minutes, at most – and before Darcy could think of something to say to this stranger he had married, they were pulling to a stop in front of the house.

Darcy was the first to disembark. He then turned and reached a hand out to assist Elizabeth down. That same frisson of feeling shot up his arm, making him breathless. His new wife's eyes darted at him briefly, but when she had both feet on the ground, she moved quickly away. Darcy shook out his hand; his fingers continued to tingle.

Elizabeth headed straight for the front door, nearly at a run. Darcy hastened to catch up, his longer legs allowing him to do so easily. Once in the house, he followed her into the drawing room, stopping nearly in the middle of the space when she did the same. When she wrapped her arms around her middle, Darcy searched his mind to find something to say that might comfort her. As he opened his mouth, Mrs. Bennet rushed into the room, shrilly calling for a servant. He cringed at her loud tone and brash words.

"Hill! Hill! The guests are about to arrive; where is the bowl of punch?" Longbourn's mistress noticed her daughter and new son-in-law standing in the center of the room. "Lizzy, what are you doing? You and Mr. Darcy must stand over here, by the door. You have to greet the guests when they enter." She urged Elizabeth to move, positioning her just so, then smiled brightly at Darcy. "You must stand beside her. There. Like that." She stepped back and clasped her hands in front of her. She sighed. "What a handsome couple you make."

Darcy cleared his throat. "Thank you, madam." He looked at Elizabeth, who remained silent.

Mrs. Bennet frowned. She moved closer and shook her finger in her daughter's face. "Do not behave all high and mighty, Miss Lizzy. You will greet those guests with a smile on your face and a kind word on your lips. You are very well settled, and far above anyone of our acquaintance. You should be grateful for this blessing. Do not make me speak to your father about your disrespect."

Elizabeth's jaw clenched, her teeth grinding loudly. She inhaled through her nose. "Thank you, Mama."

The rest of Elizabeth's family began to filter into the room, and without another word, her mother fluttered away, her attention drawn to her youngest and most beloved child.

With a roll of her eyes, Elizabeth huffed. Her arms came up once again to wrap around her.

For all his anger and resentment at the circumstances in which he found himself, Darcy felt a spark of compassion light inside at Elizabeth's situation. He was aware that she had only learned of their betrothal the day before, on her seven and tenth birthday. He had known about it for two years, since the day he turned eight and ten. Time had smoothed the roughest edges of his feelings, enabling him to see past his own emotions now. He leaned down to whisper to his wife.

"I am sorry. I tried to convince my father to speak to yours and allow us to meet before today, but he denied me."

Elizabeth turned her face to stare into his eyes. Her brows drew together, forming a crease. "You could not refuse to go through with it?"

Darcy shook his head. "I am not of age. Even if I were, my inheritance rests on this marriage, and on producing an heir." He glanced toward the door as the number of voices in the entry hall increased, the sound filtering into the drawing room where he and Elizabeth stood. He looked at his wife again. "If it were summer, I would be able to fight it. I have a small inheritance from my grandmother set aside for me, so losing Pemberley would not be a hardship, though I do love the estate. I am every bit as stuck as you, though."

Elizabeth said nothing, though her lips flattened. The elder Mr. Darcy entered the room with Mr. Bennet, approaching her and her new husband.

"Congratulations, Mr. Darcy, Lizzy." Bennet bowed to his son-in-law and daughter, then made way for Mr. George Darcy to do the same.

"Congratulations to both of you." The elder Darcy smirked. "You should enjoy the breakfast while you can. We will need to leave to return to London soon." With a shallow bow, he turned to follow Bennet to the refreshments table.

Other guests followed, and Darcy had no further opportunity to speak to Elizabeth, though he had watched a look of loathing briefly cross her face as his father walked away. *Trust me*, he thought. *I know how you feel.*

~~~***~~~

Two hours later, Darcy watched as Elizabeth tearfully hugged her sisters. The other girls
~~~

clung to her, making her promise to write and begging her to host them.

"Lydia, you and Kitty are not yet out. You must finish your education. I hope to have Jane and Mary come to me soon, but I am not going to my own home. My husband and I will live with his father, and he may not wish for visitors." When Lydia, the youngest and most spoiled of the girls, began to whine, Elizabeth immediately put a stop to it. "No. I beg you; learn everything you can so you will have some understanding of what is happening if Papa does to you what he did to me." She held Lydia's shoulders. "Listen to me. I am now married to a total stranger. I never thought something like this would happen, and I have no idea of my husband's character, nor that of his father. I am grateful for my education, because it will enable me to take care of myself, should the worst come to pass. Do you understand what I am trying to say?"

Lydia slowly nodded, her eyes wide. "I do. I will try, but do at least come to visit."

Elizabeth sighed again. "I will try." She kissed each of her sisters. Her tears, which had largely dried up while she lectured Lydia, began to flow again. "I love you. I will send my direction as soon as I can. You must write to me, too." After receiving their promises to do as she asked, Elizabeth turned, lifting her chin. With Darcy's hand cupping her elbow, she approached her parents, standing stoically as her mother wrapped her in a hug and sobbed on her shoulder. Finally released, she curtseyed. "Good bye, Mama, Papa." She turned away, striding to the door.

Darcy bowed to his in-laws, murmuring his farewell, then followed Elizabeth. Arriving at her side, he reached into his pocket and pulled out a square of linen, handing it to her. He nodded to the coachman as that man walked past. Too many servants about, he thought. It may be bedtime before I can freely speak to her again. He sighed.

George Darcy approached. "Get in," he ordered, looking up at the sky. "It will be nearly dark by the time we reach town."

Silently, Darcy held his hand out to Elizabeth. She hesitated, but then placed hers in his. He curled his fingers around her palm, assisting her in entering, then let go and followed her in. Elizabeth had chosen the front-facing seat, and Darcy paused, uncertain if she would appreciate his presence beside her. He sat on the opposite side.

"Sit beside your wife." George Darcy spoke harshly, as he always had, for as long as his son could remember.

Darcy immediately moved to sit beside Elizabeth, who scooted over and then glared at his father. He held his breath, afraid she would say something and raise the elder Darcy's ire. After a few moments, she moved her gaze to the window, and he breathed a quiet sigh of relief.

There was no discussion in the carriage on the way to London. George Darcy issued instructions when they pulled into the coaching inn to change horses, telling the young couple to do what they needed to do as far as refreshing themselves as quickly as possible and return to the carriage. Darcy objected, insisting he be allowed to procure at least some bread, cheese, and ale for Elizabeth. George Darcy grudgingly consented

When the equipage stopped, the elder Darcy exited first with the younger following. Fitzwilliam Darcy then handed Elizabeth down. He did not let go of her hand, instead using it to hold her back from following the older gentleman.

"I apologize that you must deal with my father in such close quarters." Darcy pitched his voice low, speaking quickly. "He is a hard man, and difficult to please. Please be careful how you speak to him."

Elizabeth stopped and stared at her husband as though he had grown an extra head. "Why?"

Darcy glanced toward the privy, where his father had just opened the door. "He uses harsh and hurtful language, and I would not wish for you to be subjected to his rage unnecessarily."

Elizabeth's eyes roamed his face for a moment, but then she nodded. "Very well. I will endeavor to keep my tongue in my head, at least for now."

Darcy's shoulders sagged briefly. "Thank you." He looked toward the privy once more. "I will go into the inn and ask for a basket to be made up. If you will refresh yourself now, I can have you hold the basket so I can do the same."

Elizabeth nodded. "I will do that." She squeezed Darcy's hand, which still held hers. "Thank you."

A small smile flitted across Darcy's face. "You are welcome." Another quick glance made him let go of Elizabeth. "My father is finished. He seems to be heading into the inn. Go ahead and do what you need to. I shall return as quickly as I can."

When Darcy returned with the basket, Elizabeth was seated on a bench placed alongside the inn. He set their lunch beside her, striding to the privy. A few minutes later, he returned to her side. "Come, let us get in the carriage. It would be best if we were there before my father."

Elizabeth's brow creased, but she rose and followed Darcy to the equipage. The grooms were just finishing up the harnessing of the new set of horses, but Darcy handed her up, anyway. He had no more than seated himself when his father appeared in the open doorway.

George Darcy grunted at the sight of the younger people waiting for him, but that was the only sound he made. He tapped the roof with his walking stick, and within seconds, they were in motion.

It was not until the carriage reached the outskirts of London that the elder Darcy spoke again. "I expect at least one of you to have concocted some plan or other to wait until you know each other better before you commence your marital duties. I will tell you right now, I will not have it. I expect proof of consummation to be presented to me before I retire for the night. We will eat together in the dining room first. Mrs. Bishop has her orders; there will be a meal ready for us. After that, you will proceed to your rooms and do what is expected."

Elizabeth gasped at George Darcy's pronouncement. Fitzwilliam Darcy reached for her hand, giving it a light squeeze. Neither said anything.

"I take it from your silence that you disagree with my instruction." George Darcy's mien took on a harder cast, his eyes cold. "Let me remind you, Son, that you can be replaced in my house and in my will with someone who is always willing to obey me."

Darcy's jaw clenched. He nodded once, and, through gritted teeth, responded to his father. "Yes, sir." He looked at Elizabeth, noting the flash of revulsion in her expression before she smoothed her features. He squeezed her hand again, retaining it in his grasp as he transferred his gaze to the window on his side.

Chapter 2

Sometime later, the Darcy carriage pulled up in front of a large home with a stone façade. Elizabeth's eyes widened as she peered out the window at it. It was on the tip of her tongue to ask about it, but she was still offended by her new father-in-law's crudity and elected to hold her tongue.

As at the coaching inn, George Darcy stepped out of the equipage first, followed by his son. When her husband held out his hand with a small smile, Elizabeth took it. She held her breath, waiting to see if she would experience the same rush of feeling she had every other time she touched him. She was not disappointed and the breath whooshed out of her as the expected tingle raced up her arm and straight to her heart. She swallowed when Darcy placed her hand on his arm, glancing up at him before turning her attention forward.

Elizabeth looked up as she took a step toward the house, counting the rows of windows. Five stories! Oh, my! She swallowed, her eyes wide.

Following her husband's lead, Elizabeth handed her bonnet, gloves, and pelisse to a waiting servant. She stood with hands clasped in front of her as Fitzwilliam Darcy made the introductions.

"Mrs. Darcy, may I present Mrs. Bishop. She is Darcy House's housekeeper. Beside her is Mr. Baxter. He has been the butler here as long as I can remember." Darcy paused, giving Elizabeth time to acknowledge the greetings of the servants. "Mrs. Bishop, Mr. Baxter, this is my wife, Mrs. Darcy. I believe my father intends her to act as mistress. It will be she to whom you report."

Elizabeth noted the looks that darted between the head servants, but did not know how to interpret them. When Darcy dismissed the pair before she had the opportunity to speak further to them, she frowned at him. She opened her mouth to tell him how she felt about his officiousness, but he spoke before she was able to.

"Come; let us proceed to the dining room." Finally noting Elizabeth's expression, Darcy leaned down to whisper in her ear. "They are very loyal to my father. I will explain more later."

Elizabeth bowed her head slightly to indicate she had heard. She allowed her husband to tuck her hand under his elbow again and walk her to the dining room.

Elizabeth was surprised at the seating arrangements. The table was smaller than what she expected for a house this size. George Darcy sat at one end, and the other was set with two places. Fitzwilliam Darcy assisted Elizabeth into the chair on the other end, then took a place to her right, leaving one empty place between himself and his father.

Suddenly, a servant was at Elizabeth's elbow with a plate of food covered by a silver lid. She drew back to allow him to place it before her. When he pulled off the lid, she was relieved to see a simple beef pie. She looked up, first at her husband and then her father-in-law. Not knowing how meals worked in the Darcy household, she decided to follow Fitzwilliam's lead. She gritted her teeth as the reasons for her presence in this house filled her mind once more, along with thoughts of what was to come as soon as she was finished eating. I wonder if I can dawdle long enough over my meal to prevent it happening, she thought.

Without a word, George Darcy began to eat, his son following suit.

The meal proceeded without conversation and without further courses. Though she did try to delay eating, Elizabeth's need for sustenance – she had not eaten since breaking her fast the previous day – outweighed her desire to put off the consummation of her marriage, and she quickly consumed the pie.

George Darcy had just pushed his chair back when the butler entered the room. He approached the master, leaning down to whisper something in the man's ear. With a nod, George waved the servant away again and pushed himself up and out of his chair.

"I have an unexpected guest. You may delay your presentation until morning." George Darcy leaned over the table, his fists pressing into the top and his countenance dark. "You will, however, complete the act this night. Mrs. Butler will be waiting outside your rooms for word and will take custody of the sheets." He stood, a sneer twisting his features. "Be grateful this is not medieval times." Without another word, he turned and strode out the door.

Elizabeth trembled, her jaw clenched. She was startled out of her rage by the sound of her new husband's chair scraping the floor as he pushed away from the table. She felt more than saw him move to stand behind her.

"Come, Mrs. Darcy. It is better to obey immediately." Darcy pulled on Elizabeth's chair.

Feeling the movement, Elizabeth pushed, allowing her husband to ease her away from the table. She placed her hand in the one held out to her, startling anew at the frisson that raced up her arm and across to her heart. With a glance up at Darcy, she stood and allowed him to lead her out of the dining room and up the stairs.

~~~***~~~

Upon reaching their rooms, Darcy held the door so Elizabeth could enter first. He followed her in, locking the door behind them. She stopped in the center of the opulent room, her arms wrapped around her middle.

"This is my bedchamber." Darcy appeared beside his wife, speaking softly. "It is expected for us to begin here tonight." He blushed, looking down for a moment before raising his eyes and looking around the room. He gestured to a door to their right. "My dressing room is behind this door. My valet is Smith."

Elizabeth murmured her understanding. The exercise of climbing two flights of stairs, combined with a sudden case of nerves and sheer exhaustion, had caused a large part of her rage to disperse. At this point, she just wanted to get this part of the day over with. Feeling her courage rise, she followed Darcy across the room and through another door.

"This is a sitting room we share." Darcy looked around. "It could perhaps use some re-
~~~

decorating. I will ask my father to allow you to do it, but be aware that we may have to live with it for now."

Elizabeth looked around at the ornate wallpaper and heavy furniture. "Yes, I believe you are right when you say it needs redecorated. However, it is in good shape. If your request is refused, at least we will not have wallpaper falling down on top of us."

Darcy chuckled, the first sign of levity to be seen in either of them the entirety of the day. He gestured toward the far side of the room. "Your bedchamber is through this door." He led his wife across the small room, pushing open the wooden panel and guiding her through.

Elizabeth stepped into the chamber, eyeing the elegant but dark walls done in a hunter green. She noted the tall window with its heavy drapes, and the large canopied bed taking up most of the floor space. "It is rather dark."

"Yes." Darcy looked around at the walls. "This entire suite is rather dark. If you like, I will see if Father will allow all three rooms to be decorated."

Elizabeth nodded. She noticed another door. "Does this lead to my dressing room?"

"Yes." Darcy strode past her, opening the portal so Elizabeth could go through.

Allowing her gaze to roam, Elizabeth noted the copper tub in front of the fireplace, and the set of double doors that led to a smaller room, where she could see her trunks sitting on the floor. On the other end of the dressing room, between the fireplace and the door to the hallway, were arranged a chaise lounge and a small table with two chairs.

"We will not be here long this trip. If you do not like it here, perhaps we can persuade my father to allow us to remain at Pemberley, our estate, and not come to London at all." Darcy looked toward the fireplace. "Sadly, there are no guarantees."

A noise from the sitting room caught the couple's attention, and Darcy swiftly stepped through Elizabeth's bedroom to the shared space. Elizabeth trotted to keep up.

"Bathwater is being prepared, sir."

"Very good." Darcy motioned for Elizabeth to step up beside him. "Mrs. Darcy, this is my valet, Mr. Smith. I wish for the two of you to become acquainted, because Smith will be your likeliest source for information when I am unavailable."

Elizabeth nodded. "Thank you." She moved her eyes to take in the tall, wiry man with the touch of grey at his temples. "I am pleased to make your acquaintance, Mr. Smith."

Smith bowed. "Likewise, madam. I have taken the liberty of suggesting Jenny Malone for the position of lady's maid." He looked at Darcy. "She is a trustworthy young lady who trained under my sister."

"Excellent. You may tell her to bring up Mrs. Darcy's bathwater when you bring mine."

Smith inclined his head. "Very good, sir." He paused. "I should tell you, Mrs. Bishop –"

Darcy interrupted. "Is impatiently waiting outside the door?" When Smith affirmed his guess, Darcy rolled his eyes. "Very well, then. You are dismissed. I will ring when we are ready for baths."

Elizabeth watched the servant go, suddenly aflutter inside. The time had come. A surge of something welled up from her stomach, causing her chin to lift.

When Darcy reached for her hand, Elizabeth gave it to him. He raised it to his lips and kissed it, and fire licked the spot his lips had touched, radiating heat that engulfed her hand and raced up her arm.

"I must first say that I am sorry you are in this position. It was a shock to me, as well, and I have spent the last two years trying to figure out a way out of it." Darcy searched her eyes. "I will try not to hurt you, this night or in the future. My father would call me weak, but I do not wish to be overbearing like he is."

Elizabeth's gaze bore into Darcy's. She saw the earnestness in his look and realized how powerless he must feel. "Thank you." She thought she ought to say more, but this man was a stranger and she was not prone to baring her soul to people she did not know.

"I would like to kiss you. You do not have to consent, but it may help you relax."

Darcy had moved closer and lifted one hand to brush Elizabeth's cheek. Feelings she had never experienced and did not understand swept over her. Suddenly, she very much wished for his kiss. She nodded, followed by a squeaky, "Yes."

Darcy closed the gap between them, brushing his lips over Elizabeth's. Soon, his arms wrapped around her, bringing her tight to his body. His tongue darted out to lick the seam of her lips and when she opened for him, he moaned into her mouth. He picked her up, carrying her to the bed and laying her down upon it.

~~~***~~~
~~~

An indeterminate amount of time later, Darcy and Elizabeth lay in bed, sweaty and out of breath, with her head upon his shoulder and his arm around her. Elizabeth felt Darcy kiss her forehead. She swallowed and closed her eyes.

"Is it always like this?"

Darcy's chuckle rumbled through his chest. "Wonderful? It can be. I hope it will be." He lifted his head to look at her, a crease forming between his brows. "Was it wonderful for you?"

Elizabeth tilted her head up to meet his eyes. "Unexpectedly, yes." She turned bright red. "It did hurt for a brief moment, but after that, it was … quite … lovely." She sputtered to a stop.

"I am sorry I had to cause you pain. I did my best to alleviate it." Darcy brought his free hand up to stroke Elizabeth's cheek.

"Do not fret. It was brief." She nuzzled Darcy's palm, her eyes closed. A wave of embarrassment overwhelmed her and she turned her face into his chest. "I am so ashamed of how utterly wild I was."

"Do not be." Darcy used his bent forefinger to gently lift Elizabeth's face so he could see it. "We are married, forever united. We are also strangers, and if this –" He waved his hand over them and the bed. "Is enjoyable, it will give us a foundation of sorts. We are clearly compatible here. With time, I am certain we can grow to like each other very much. Or, even, to love each other."

Elizabeth bit her lip but nodded. "Yes, it is good we are well-matched here. In normal circumstances, I would disagree with the thought of bedroom activities being a decent foundation for a marriage, but our circumstances are far from normal."

Darcy ran his hand up and down Elizabeth's arm. "They are not normal at all." He shot a glance at the hallway door. "What say we make Mrs. Bishop wait out there a bit longer?" He rolled to face his wife, his free hand diving under the covers to rub over her bottom.

Suddenly breathless, Elizabeth pressed herself closer to Darcy. "Yes, we should do that."

Darcy pressed his lips to Elizabeth's, and soon, all thought of the woman in the hallway was gone.

~~~***~~~

The next morning, Elizabeth blinked awake to the feel of a large, warm body behind hers and a heavy weight across her waist. She looked around, remembering that she and Darcy had finished their night in her bedroom, after he had allowed Mrs. Bishop into his room to inspect
~~~

the sheets and remove them. Bathwater had been brought up; the couple had dressed for the night, and then made the decision to sleep in her bed rather than his, if for no other reason than to stymie the servants.

Chapter 3

The sun was just beginning to rise over the city of London. Elizabeth lay quietly, thinking back over the previous night. I remain angry, she thought, but the deed is done. I am well and truly married, and marriage is forever. She sighed. Fitzwilliam Darcy has treated me gently so far, and my body responds strongly to him. She blushed at the memory of the activities they had engaged in and how easily he had been able to make her forget everything else. Her muscles stiffened and her brow creased as she recalled the argument with her father two mornings ago, after he informed her of her upcoming wedding. Her stomach felt tied in knots, a feeling she hated. I despise being unhappy; I am not formed for it. I must eventually deal with my father and his duplicity, but for now, I wish to find a way to be happy in my marriage. I must get to know my husband and learn to esteem and respect him.

Elizabeth's thoughts turned to her new father-in-law. She shuddered at the memory of his sneer, and his insistence that she and his son not only perform their marital duties but also show him the dirtied bedding. He is a disgusting person. Hopefully, we will not need to be in his presence often.

Elizabeth felt Darcy stir behind her, his arm tightening around her middle. She looked over her shoulder. "Good morning."

"Good morning." Darcy kissed Elizabeth's shoulder, then her neck when she laid her head down to give him access, and finally, her head. "I should enjoy making love to you again, but we need to be on the road soon. We are going to my father's estate in Scotland for our wedding trip, and I would like to make as much progress today as possible." He paused. "Before we leave, I will need to show him our evidence. I apologize."

Elizabeth was quiet for a moment, but then asked the question she had wanted an answer to last night. "Why did he do it?"

"Insist on consummation?"

When Elizabeth nodded her head, Darcy continued.

"I do not know why. He was not always this way. I remember a far kinder man when my mother was alive. He was strict, and even harsh at times, but never unkind as he is now. He is frightening sometimes." Darcy paused. "He has been known to throw things and to strike walls. I have often feared for my safety." He felt down Elizabeth's arm to her hand, twining their fingers together. "After Mama passed away, he brought me to London with him and left me with the nanny and my tutors. He began staying out all night and coming home intoxicated." Darcy shrugged.

"I was occupied with tutors and masters until I was six and ten, when I went up to Cambridge. On my eighteenth birthday, I was summoned to Darcy House and informed that I had been betrothed to you three years previously. I did everything I could think of to get it nullified, even going so far as to put myself in danger, but my father refused to relent. He had become more and more difficult to bear. Then, he told me that if I would not marry you, he would. I could not do that to you. I would not have been able to live with myself had I allowed a stranger to be forced into marriage with him." Darcy leaned away from Elizabeth and rolled her to her back. "I promise I will protect you from him as much as I am able. We will be alone on our wedding trip and I will be able to explain things further. In the meantime, except for Smith, trust no one. The rest of the servants are fiercely loyal to my father and will not hesitate to report our movements to him."

Elizabeth frowned. "What about my maid?"

Darcy hesitated, looking over her shoulder for a moment as he considered the new servant.

"Smith indicated her trustworthiness last night. I will speak to him to assure myself of it, but in the meantime, do not confide in her. If she turns out to be loyal to you and not Father, you can change that behavior." He paused, looking into Elizabeth's eyes and caressing her cheek with his hand. "I know it will be difficult to trust me right away. To be honest, it is difficult to trust you. We are total strangers. However, if we are to survive, we would be better together than apart."

Elizabeth had given Darcy her entire attention while he spoke and now nodded. "I agree." She paused. "My courage always rises with every attempt to intimidate me. I will follow your lead with your father, because you know him best, but I will not allow him to cow me."

Darcy smiled softly at his wife. Then, he leaned over and gently caressed her lips with his own. "Come, then; let us rise and begin our day."

~~~***~~~

One half hour later, Darcy knocked on the door to his father's study, the sheet from his bed in his hand. Upon hearing the elder Darcy's command to enter, he pressed the latch down and pushed the wood panel inward.
~~~

"You wished to see me this morning, sir." Darcy approached his father's desk, behind which sat the man himself.

George Darcy looked up from the ledger he was perusing. "I understand you attempted to avoid this appointment." He stared at his son, his eyes drilling into the younger man's.

Fitzwilliam Darcy felt his blood begin to pound. He clenched his jaw but strove to keep his countenance smooth. "Not on purpose, sir. I could not find Mrs. Bishop to obtain the sheet."

George sat back, eyeing Darcy up and down. Finally, he spoke. "Unfurl it so I may examine it."

Feeling heat rising up his neck under his cravat, Fitzwilliam Darcy did as he was commanded, unfolding the linen and holding it up so the stains showed. He remained silent, his skin crawling, waiting for his father to speak. He swallowed down the nausea that threatened to overtake him. *This is not the first time he has humiliated me so,* he thought. *Soon, it will be over. Be patient.*

"Where is your wife?"

"She is waiting in the dining room for me." Darcy glared at his father over the top of the sheet.

George Darcy nodded at his son's information. He said nothing for a long moment. Finally, he waved his hand over the desk. "You may send that to be washed. You have saved a part of your inheritance. Congratulations." His voice was flat. "I expect a pregnancy within a six-month, else I will be forced to hand over Pemberley to my godson. He is far more obedient than you, and better equipped to do what is necessary to keep it running."

Gritting his teeth, Darcy replied. "I understand." He struggled to keep his hands at his sides; what he wanted to do was wrap them around himself. He blinked back the tears he felt forming in his eyes.

"You are dismissed." George Darcy turned his attention back to his ledger.

With a tipping of his head and nothing else, Fitzwilliam Darcy spun on his heel and stalked out the door. Every muscle rigid, he marched down the stairs and into the dining room. He paused upon entering, closing his eyes and breathing deeply. He heard the scrape of a chair and soon felt a gentle hand on his arm.

"Are you well?"

Elizabeth's soft voice was a balm to Darcy's soul. He swallowed, opening his eyes. "I will be."

Elizabeth squeezed his arm briefly, then walked to the door to address the footman in the hall. She returned to her husband's side. "I have called for Mr. Smith. I will have him take that to the laundry." She gestured to the sheet bunched in Darcy's hand.

With a start, Darcy looked down. "I had forgotten I had this. I apologize."

Just then, Smith entered and bowed. "You requested me, madam?"

"Yes, I did." Elizabeth nodded to Darcy's burden. "Please take that to the laundry." She glanced at her husband. "I understand we are leaving soon. I should like to be gone now. Is the carriage readied, and can you pack us up a basket? I fear Mr. Darcy has not had time to break his fast this morning."

Smith looked at Darcy and, upon receiving his nod, bowed to Elizabeth. "Certainly, madam. I believe the horses are being hitched as we speak." He reached for the bundle. "I will deliver this to the laundress and come back. By the time you are ready to get into the coach, I will have a basket for you."

Darcy listened to his wife and valet speak as he fought to overcome his feelings. When Smith had the sheet in his hands and bowed, Darcy dismissed him, but not before a look passed between them in which he allowed his eyes to express his gratitude. Judging by the small lift of the servant's lips, his message was received.

As soon as they were alone again, Elizabeth spoke to Darcy. "I am sorry for taking over. I know I should have waited for you, but you were so distressed that I wished to ease your burden."

Darcy smiled weakly. "I do not mind. In fact, I am grateful. I, too, wish to be gone from here as soon as possible." He turned, offering Elizabeth his arm. "If you are ready, we can wait in the entry hall."

"I am." Elizabeth tucked her hand under Darcy's elbow and allowed him to lead her to the front door. There the couple waited silently while servants brought their trunks down.

When the coach and four pulled to a stop in front of the house, Darcy led his wife down the steps and assisted her into the equipage. He entered behind her, and, true to his word, Smith appeared before the footman could shut the door, a small basket with a cloth covering it in one hand and a flagon of cider in the other. Darcy accepted the items, placing them between himself and Elizabeth. With a nod, the valet shut the door. Darcy turned to look out the back window, watching as Smith handed Jenny into the smaller carriage behind them. He faced forward once again and tapped the roof with his walking stick. The coach lurched into motion.

Neither Darcy nor Elizabeth spoke as they rumbled through the London streets. He reached for her hand, gratified that she turned hers over to clasp his.

Eventually, the rough cobblestones of the city made way for the often-rutted dirt of the road headed north. The further away from London they travelled, the easier Darcy breathed. With a squeeze of Elizabeth's hand, he let it go. "Shall we see what Smith packed for us?"

"Oh, yes. I confess I did not eat very much this morning, but I am ravenous now." Elizabeth smiled and reached for the cloth covering their breakfast. "It looks like we have scones." She poked around the inside of the basket. "There are two small pots in here; I would guess one is jam, but the contents of the other are yet a mystery. I do smell beef. There must be bread in here, as well."

"Why do we not begin with the scones?" Darcy removed his gloves, tucking them into his pocket. He accepted the two small pots Elizabeth handed him, setting one on the seat between his leg and the basket. He opened the pot in his hand. "Yes, jam. Mmm." He replaced the lid and set the jar down, picking up the other one. "Clotted cream. A bit messy for in the carriage, but we will manage."

"We will be careful." Elizabeth handed him the cloth that had covered the basket. "Scoot over and lay this out. We can use it like a picnic blanket."

When Darcy had done as she had instructed, Elizabeth handed him two scones. "One for each of us. There are two more, if you are still hungry when we are finished." She pulled a pair of utensils out of the basket.

Between the two of them, Darcy and Elizabeth managed to spread the jam and cream over the scones. They sat back against the squabs and savored the delicious treat. Then, Darcy poured them each a cup of cider. By the time they finished their drinks and got the basket packed back up again, the coach was nearing the next posting station. Darcy looked out the window, seeing familiar landmarks.

"We will be stopping to change horses again within the half hour. If you do not mind, I would like this to be a brief stop. Just change the horses, use the privy, and be on our way." Darcy looked at his hands for a moment, then back up at his wife. "The further from my father we are, the happier I will be."

Elizabeth tilted her head. "I agree. We still have the beef and bread in the basket. We can eat that if we get hungry again." She paused. "Scotland is several days from London."

"Yes." Darcy lips rose briefly. "It takes a full seven days, usually, but the weather is fine, and if we make only brief stops, we may shorten the time."

"We have plenty of time to talk, then, even if we do make the trip faster." Elizabeth looked down. "I should like to get to know you better."

Darcy lifted one corner of his lips into a smile. "I would like the same in regards to you."

Conversation ceased as the coach began to slow. The moment it came to a stop, Darcy opened the door, descended, and handed Elizabeth out. They made their way to the privy at the back of the posting house, used it, entered the coach again, and were back on the road within five minutes.

Darcy fidgeted for a couple minutes as the equipage began to pick up speed. Uncertain how to begin the conversation, he frantically searched his mind for something to say. Inspiration struck when he recalled the book he had tucked into his pocket that morning. "Do you enjoy reading, Mrs. Darcy?"

Elizabeth turned her gaze from the window to her husband. "I do not mind if you call me by my Christian name." She blushed. "When we are alone, anyway." She paused. "I love to read. Do you?"

Darcy smiled. "I do … Elizabeth." He pulled the small book of Shakespeare's sonnets out of his pocket. "You will find I am never without a book. This one is Shakespeare. Perhaps we might read aloud to each other when we tire of conversation."

Elizabeth's lips twitched. "Perhaps we may. Which of the Bard's works is that?"" She craned her neck to try to see the title.

"It is the sonnets. I greatly enjoy his poetry, though I like his histories more. This volume is small enough to carry everywhere, so I often find myself revisiting it."

Elizabeth nodded. "Very wise. I also enjoy poetry. I have read all of Shakespeare's plays. I like the histories, and even, at times, the tragedies, but I much prefer the comedies." She looked down. "I have always loved a laugh."

Darcy's heart squeezed in his chest. He laid his hand over his wife's. "I am sure you do not feel much like laughing at this point." He ducked his head down to try to see her face. "I hope you will one day wish to do so again." He gripped her hand tightly. "We may not have wished for this union, but I will have you know that I have vowed to do my best to make you happy and to have a good marriage."

Elizabeth finally looked up. Though her lips turned downward, she attempted to lift one corner into a smile. "Thank you." She took a deep breath, briefly closing her eyes and opening them again. "I decided early this morning, right before you awoke, that I would do the same. I am not formed for unhappiness, though admittedly, I have never been in such an awkward and sometimes horrible position. I will be myself again. Eventually."

Darcy's gaze wandered Elizabeth's features for a moment. He then pulled her close, releasing her hand to wrap his arm around her shoulders and draw her to his chest. He felt her resist momentarily, but before he could react, she had settled against him. He felt her hand move and within seconds, she was pulling her bonnet off. He kissed her head as she relaxed further against him. They remained in that position, silent but drawing and giving comfort, until both fell asleep.

Chapter 4

Darcy and Elizabeth remained asleep until the coach stopped at the next posting station. As before, they used the privy and got back in the equipage, which immediately pulled out of the yard and back onto the roadway.

"I am hungry. What say we eat that beef now?" Darcy reached across to the other seat and picked up the basket.

"Yes, let us do that." Elizabeth pressed a hand to her stomach. "I did not realize how hungry I was until you mentioned it."

"We shall have to take more time at the next stop so we can at least get another basket." Darcy set up their dining area, laying the cloth on the seat between them, then laying out the slices of bread and meat.

"We will. I confess a cup of tea would be lovely." Elizabeth removed her bonnet and gloves and peeked inside the basket. "There are two scones left."

"Dessert." Darcy grinned up at his wife, then moved the basket to the other seat. "Dinner is served, madam."

"Thank you, sir." Elizabeth placed a slice of beef between two slices of bread.

"You are very welcome." Darcy followed his wife's lead, and soon was devouring his meal. When he finished, he prepared another scone for each of them and poured the rest of the cider into the two cups.

"Your first name is Fitzwilliam?" Elizabeth sipped her cider.

"It is. Fitzwilliam is my mother's maiden name." Darcy paused, taking a bite of scone and chewing while he considered what to say. "Mother's brother is the current Earl of Matlock. He is not as harsh as my father, but he is not warm and friendly, either. He is a stickler for propriety. I do not see him often, but when I do, he always makes me feel inadequate." He shrugged. "I do not really like my first name, but it is what it is."

Elizabeth watched Darcy speak, her brow furrowed at the thought of his apparent lack of loving relations. "I am sorry. Have you ever shortened it? I could call you William, if you prefer?"

Darcy gave Elizabeth a crooked smile. "I do not mind if you shorten it to William. Just please not Fitz; my schoolmates called me that and I hated it."

"William it is, then." Elizabeth smiled. She finished her scone and cider, handing the cup back to Darcy. "What does your father call you?"

Darcy's features darkened. "'Son' is the most polite name he has given me. He does occasionally call me Fitzwilliam." He paused and thought for a long moment. "It might be best to remain formal in our address to each other in front of him. If he thinks we are becoming close, he might do or say something to cause discord between us." He tucked the remains of the meal back into the basket and set it on the other seat.

Elizabeth sighed but agreed. "Will we be in his presence often?"

Darcy shrugged. "It is hard to say." He sat back and wrapped his arm around his wife's shoulders, as he had before. "I was at Cambridge until just a few weeks ago, and only saw him during school breaks. Now that I have completed my studies, there really is no way to know what he expects as far as our living arrangements. We will have to enjoy the days we have away and do our best to survive the rest of the time."

Elizabeth remained silent as she digested this information. "Have you no siblings?"

"I have a sister. She is eight. Father left her at Pemberley with her governess."

"I see. My youngest sister just turned one and ten." Elizabeth snuggled into Darcy's side. The day had turned a bit chilly, not unusual for early May. "You said your mother has passed on. How old were you when you lost her?"

Darcy absently rubbed his hand up and down Elizabeth's arm. "Mama died when I was two and ten."

Elizabeth was quiet for so long, Darcy had begun to think she had fallen asleep again. He was startled when she spoke.

"If you are not of age, how old are you?"

"I am twenty."

Elizabeth nodded, her cheek rubbing Darcy's waistcoat. "I believe you know I am seven and ten." She paused, hearing Darcy's quiet murmur. "My father called me into his book room on my birthday. He told me he had a story to tell me, and some information I needed to know." She bit her lip, reliving the event in her mind. "It seems my mother made herself very ill when I was two and ten, worrying about the entail that is in place on my father's estate. She had five daughters and had suffered three miscarriages since my youngest sister was born. When she realized that more children were not likely to come, she allowed fear to overcome her. She became very ill; the physician thought she would die.

"Papa sent a letter to my uncle in London, asking him to find husbands for my elder sister, Jane, and me. Uncle Gardiner found you for me, but Mama insisted on a peer for Jane. After five years, she still is not engaged, as far as I know." It was Elizabeth's turn to shrug. "I threw an absolute fit when I found out. However, Papa insisted I obey him; he said the knowledge that I will marry well is all that keeps Mama from descending into her illness again."

"He used your mother's health to persuade you to go along with the plan willingly." Darcy's soft murmur was followed by a kiss to his wife's hair. "Was he kind to you, growing up?"

Elizabeth whispered into Darcy's waistcoat. "I was his favorite. He taught me himself. Mathematics, reading, philosophy, Latin, even history. Looking back, I can see that he mocked me every bit as much as he did my mother and sisters. He called us all silly, though I remember hearing him tell Mama recently that I had something more of quickness than the others did." She clung to Darcy's waist, both arms encompassing it.

"Do you think he regrets his choice?" Darcy wrapped his free arm around Elizabeth, holding her tighter.

"I hope he does." Elizabeth's voice became hard. "I hope one day his freedom to choose is stripped away, as he did mine." She sniffed. "I know the church teaches to forgive, and normally, I am able to do so quickly, but I do not know that I can this time." She looked up at Darcy. "I do not wish to hurt you. I find I like you very much and have great hopes for our happiness as a couple. However, he could not know ahead of time that we would suit. We were not even given the chance to court." She rested her head against her husband's shoulder once more. "I will have to forgive him at some point, but for right now, I cannot find it in me to do so."

"I understand that." Darcy leaned his cheek on Elizabeth's head. "I feel the same about my father, but where you have this one incident that follows a lifetime of favor, I have a lifetime of disdain toward me to overcome." He closed his eyes. "I can speak no more of it today. Forgive me. I promise I will tell you all at some point, but not today."

"Think of the past only as it gives you pleasure. That has been my motto my whole life. Perhaps we need to practice it now." Elizabeth squeezed her husband's waist.

Darcy smiled. "I like the sound of that." He tipped his wife's face upward with his forefinger under her chin. "I would very much like to kiss you again."

Elizabeth blushed but smiled. "I would very much like for you to do so."

Darcy's smile slowly grew as he lowered his head. His heart pounded as he closed in on Elizabeth's lips. He brushed his mouth against hers once, then again, before settling his lips on her full, red ones. He deepened the kiss, swamping his senses in the feel of his wife. His tongue darted out, seeking and being granted entrance to her mouth. He moaned, holding her tighter.

The couple kissed until they were out of breath, then began again. They passed the remainder of the day alternately kissing, talking about their childhoods and experiences, reading from the book of sonnets, and playing games.

~~~***~~~

At the last stop for the day, Darcy escorted Elizabeth to their chambers. The innkeeper had been very accommodating, not blinking twice when Darcy requested their meals be brought up on a tray.

When the man had left, Elizabeth opened her mouth to speak to Darcy but was interrupted by Smith's knock on the door.

"Do you need anything, sir?"

Darcy shook his head. "Not at the moment, though we will later. We plan to dine here; once
~~~

finished, we will be ready for you." He looked at Elizabeth. "Would you like a bath?"

Elizabeth's eyes widened. "Oh. No, I will be fine with just a ewer of warm water. I would not wish to put the innkeeper out."

"Are you certain? My father pays a great deal for good service; the innkeeper will not think less of you for asking for bathwater."

Elizabeth hesitated a moment, but then re-iterated her reply. "No, I am happy to just wash up. I can wait a night or two to bathe."

"Very well, then." Darcy turned back to Smith. "Go downstairs and eat for now. Check back in an hour."

Smith bowed. "Very good." He stepped out of the room, shutting the door behind him.

Darcy removed his gloves and hat, setting them on the top of the dresser that took up one wall of the room. He walked over to Elizabeth, who had not moved from her position since enter-ing the chamber. He pulled on one of her bonnet strings, untying it. "Are you well?"

"I am, I think." Elizabeth looked down. "I have never spent the night at an inn before." She peeked up at him as he pulled her bonnet off and reached for her hands.

Darcy paused, Elizabeth's bonnet under one arm and his hand holding hers. "Never? Really?" His brows rose when she shook her head.

"Never. The furthest I travelled was to London. I have always slept in my bed at Longbourn, or at my uncle's house in Gracechurch Street." Elizabeth watched as Darcy proceeded to pull her gloves off, finger by finger.

"Well, you are in for a treat, then." Darcy winked when Elizabeth looked up at him. "This is a particularly good inn, else my father and uncle would never stay here. There are the typical behaviors that occur at all inns, and the walls are thin, so we may hear the snores and other noises our fellow travelers make, but the beds are especially comfortable and the food is excellent." He tucked her gloves into her bonnet and set it on the dresser beside his hat, then returned to her side and grasped her hands again. "I forgot until a few minutes ago, but I had told you I would speak to Smith about Jenny."

"You did. What is his verdict?" Elizabeth held tightly to Darcy's large, warm hands. As always when they touched, sparks flew up her arms, making her heart race.

"He said she is trustworthy. She had heard a little about my father from Smith's sister, and when he interviewed her prior to suggesting her to Mrs. Bishop, he questioned her closely on her ability to be loyal to her mistress in the face of pressure from my father to report on what happens in our suite and with you. He believes she will remain loyal to you and will follow his lead in handling my father."

Elizabeth let out a huge breath. "Good, good. I am glad to hear it. I would hate to have to be distrustful of someone who served me so intimately."

"Yes, I would, as well. Smith has become somewhat of a confidante for me in the last few years. He is frequently interrogated by my father as to my activities, but either fabricates details or makes implications." Darcy shrugged. "I do not know how Father has not caught on, but he has not."

"How long has Smith been in your employ?"

Before Darcy could respond, someone knocked on the door. He hastened over, and called through the wooden pane, "Who is it?"

"Your supper, sir."

Immediately, Darcy opened the door. A young lady who looked no older than Elizabeth stepped in, laden with a large tray with two covered plates, two cups, silverware, and the makings for tea on it. She carefully balanced the tray on the edge of the small table in the room, removing the items and arranging them for ease of use. Then, she curtseyed, accepted the coin Darcy offered her, and left the room. Darcy shut the door behind her. When he turned around, Elizabeth was standing beside one of the chairs. He hastened across the room to pull it out for her, then seated himself.

"Mmm, this is delicious." Elizabeth dipped her fork back into the meat pie and brought up another bite.

"I agree. It is always excellent here." Darcy dug into his meal.

The pair spent the next few minutes eating. It was not until they had both pushed back their plates and fixed their tea that the topic of Smith's employment was revisited.

"You were telling me about your valet." Elizabeth lifted her cup with both hands, her elbows on the table.

Darcy sat back in his seat, one hand on his hip and the other holding his tea. "Yes, I was. He was hired when my father brought me to London after my mother passed."

"He has been with you for eight or nine years?" Elizabeth sat up, removing her elbows from the table and setting the cup down.

"About that, yes." Darcy set his tea cup on the table. He played with the handle. "I do not know why, but he seemed so … sympathetic to my situation from the beginning. He never said a word to my father about any of my boyhood indiscretions, unlike my tutor, who reported every infraction."

Elizabeth stretched her hand out to lay it over Darcy's. "I am sorry. That was a terrible way to grow up. I might be angry with my parents now, but I never felt alone, not like you did."

Darcy let go of the tea cup, turning his hand so that his palm faced Elizabeth's. He intertwined their fingers, staring at them while he spoke. "Thank you." He opened his mouth as though to say more but then closed it again and remained silent. The pair sat in this attitude for a long while, only moving when Smith knocked on the door.

An hour later, Darcy and Elizabeth had both been readied for bed. Elizabeth had been attended to first, and now sat in a chair in front of the low-burning fire, her attention caught by the dancing flames. Darcy emerged in a nightshirt and dressing gown and paused to observe her. As his eyes roamed over her profile and down to the long braid that lay over her shoulder, his heart swelled. I care for her already, he thought. I hesitate to call it love, and certainly, lust plays a part in it, but it definitely is there. I no longer feel so alone; perhaps it is simply gratitude. Whatever it is, I am eager to see where our relationship goes.

Just then, Elizabeth looked up and toward Darcy's position in front of the dressing room door. She smiled, and his body came alert. He approached, his hand extended in invitation and, to his delight, she placed hers within and allowed him to help her rise.

"Elizabeth," Darcy whispered, pulling her into his arms. He kissed her and, feeling her respond, bent to tuck his arm under her knees and pick her up. He carried her to the bed, where he laid her down atop the turned-back covers and crawled in beside her.

Chapter 5

Elizabeth woke the next morning to Darcy whispering in her ear. She could see through the crack in the curtains that the sky was barely beginning to lighten. She blinked, confused at first as to her location. Stretching, she felt her husband's solid presence behind her and the kiss he placed on her neck. She suddenly felt his touches as he ran his hands over her body, and she closed her eyes and relaxed.

Later, still cradled in Darcy's arms, Elizabeth felt a little embarrassed as she recalled the noises she had heard in the night, as well as the ones she was sure she had made. She was happy to rise when her husband suggested it and break her fast out of a basket in the carriage.

~~~***~~~

The couple spent another long day in the coach. Though they occupied themselves with reading, napping, and playing games, much of their day was spent talking. They engaged in long discussions about philosophy, and debated some of the bills currently being presented before Parliament. They spoke of their childhoods, telling tales of exploits they had gotten away
~~~

with, and things they had done that had been discovered. They also discussed their siblings.

"You have four sisters?" Darcy was leaning back against the squabs, his booted feet stretched across the carriage to rest on the bench on the other side. Elizabeth leaned against him, head on his shoulder, her arms wrapped around his waist, and his around her.

"I do. Jane is the eldest and most beautiful."

Darcy thought a moment. "She stood up with you."

Elizabeth smiled. "She did. Her serenity was helpful in calming me through the worst of that morning, as well as the night before."

"I can see how that would be possible." Darcy absently kissed Elizabeth's head. "How much older is she?"

"Two years or so. She turns nineteen next month."

"Your mother wishes her to marry a peer?"

Elizabeth sighed. "So it seems. She put each of us out when we turned fifteen. I always wondered why she was so determined to marry us off, yet refused to allow us to form attachments with the gentlemen who attended the assemblies." Her brow creased. "I rather wonder at her pushing us out at all. She knew I was engaged."

"Perhaps she did it as a safeguard, in case your uncle could not broker a marriage for Jane or something happened to me." Darcy laid his cheek on Elizabeth's head.

"That may be correct. It would be like Mama to keep as many avenues as possible open."

"Mmm." Darcy paused. "Which of the sisters is next after you?"

"That would be Mary. She will turn fifteen in the autumn. She dominated the pianoforte at the wedding breakfast."

"Ah, yes. Rather fond of dark pieces." Darcy smirked when he heard Elizabeth groan.

"She is." Elizabeth shrugged. "I think she is attempting to distinguish herself from the rest of us. Mama laments all the time that Mary is not prettier, and I think it has left my sister believing she is ugly and undesirable. I have heard the same thing my whole life, because no one is more beautiful than Jane, but it did not affect me the way it has Mary."

"Does she have other accomplishments? She did not look any different than you or the rest of your sisters. Maybe she simply has not yet matured into her looks?"

"My Aunt Gardiner has said exactly that. In another year or two, Mary will blossom and be just as beautiful as Jane, though in her own way."

"Has your father asked your uncle to broker Mary's marriage, as well?" Darcy closed his eyes.

"I do not know. I was in too much shock about my own situation to ask about hers. I suspect the pressure in her case will not be as strong, given our union, but I do not know." Elizabeth peeked up, seeing his eyes were closed and one side of his lips pulled down.

Darcy's eyes popped open as something occurred to him. "Have you seen the settlement?"

Elizabeth tilted her head up once more. "No. I do not know if Papa intended to explain it to me or not, but I was too enraged to hear him if he had tried. I assume you have?"

"Yes, I had to sign it and refused to do so until I had read it through." Darcy closed his eyes once more, picturing the document in his mind. "You have your dowry, which is one thousand pounds, but you will not receive that until after your mother's death. Your father has set you an additional one hundred pounds a year during his lifetime, and your uncle gifted you one thousand pounds, to be invested in the four percents. My father is to provide pin money equal to double the interest of your dowry, and should I die first, you are to have lifetime use of the estate my grandmother left to me."

Elizabeth was silent for a long moment as she absorbed this information. When she thought she understood, she started asking questions. "Does this mean my entire dowry is safe from being used? It is set aside for my own use?"

Darcy nodded, his cheek rubbing the top of her head. "It is, all of it."

Elizabeth pulled her lips between her teeth as she thought of her next question and how to ask it without appearing rude or grasping. "You said your father is the source of my pin money. What happens to it when he dies?"

Darcy squeezed Elizabeth briefly. "It is my intention, at that point, to add to the document. I wish to raise the amount of your pin money and add to the amount of your dowry. It is contingent upon my inheritance, though." Here, he paused, biting his lip. When he spoke again, it was with marked hesitancy. "I was informed the morning we left London that I must get you with child within a six month, or forfeit part of my inheritance to my father's godson. That is not the reason I have wished to do my duty with you so often; I would desire you regardless, and would act on it as often as you would allow me." He blushed.

Elizabeth rolled her eyes. "I am happy to hear it." She paused, smirking when Darcy chuckled. "I appreciate that you told me this now. It is far better to hear it from you than to have it come from another source. Thank you for showing me respect."

"I will endeavor to always behave honorably and gentlemanly toward you." Darcy was quiet for a while, thinking about her words. "I have not had any models of marriage, other than the earl and countess. I was too young to understand anything of my parents' relationship. I am learning how to be a husband as I go, but it makes sense to me that if we communicate things to each other, our road will be much smoother than if we do not." He chewed his lip for a moment. "I am known for being reticent, so you may have to help me along."

"I am also learning as I go. You saw how my parents behaved. Mama is silly and Papa laughs at her. There is no respect between them, at least not on my father's part. I do not wish to live like that the rest of my life. Being treated with respect and esteem is important to me, as is being able to feel those things toward my husband." Elizabeth moved her head so she could once again see Darcy's expression. "So, I agree with you that we must communicate. I will assist you all that I am able to, as far as remembering to talk to each other goes."

Darcy squeezed her close. "Thank you." He cleared his throat. He began to speak again just as the coach began to slow. "I was going to ask you about your youngest sisters, but we must be approaching the inn. We shall have to put them off for a while."

Elizabeth sat up and began to straighten her clothes. "There is not much to tell about them." She laughed when the coach jerked to a stop and she was thrown forward. It was only Darcy's quick reflexes that prevented her from falling off the seat. "Thank you. I should have been holding onto something."

Darcy grinned. "I am glad you did not." He wrapped his arms around his wife once more, leaning in for a kiss. "I will take any excuse I can find for this," he whispered as his lips captured hers.

<center>~~~***~~~</center>

Darcy and Elizabeth spent another five days on the road, finally arriving at the Darcy estate in Scotland a week to the day after they married. It was late when the coach and four pulled into the gate, the early evening sun casting long shadows.

Darcy nodded to the footman as he descended from inside the carriage, then turned to hand Elizabeth out.

Elizabeth smiled at Darcy as she stepped to the ground, then looked up at the house, a large, stone building with a wing on either end. A door was open at the end of the main portion of the home, and servants poured out, climbing over the carriage to retrieve the luggage and scurry back into the house with it. She turned to Darcy with a smile. "It is an adorable house."

Darcy chuckled. "If you like this view, you will love the front." He tipped his head toward the line of servants. "It is easier to unload here, so we always do, but for our day to day needs, we will use the front door."

"I look forward to it." Elizabeth shivered as the sun dropped behind the house, taking much of the day's warmth with it. "Brrr. It is rather cold here."

Darcy startled from his observations of the house and footmen. "I am sorry. Come; let us go inside. We will sit in front of a fire while we wait for supper." He tucked Elizabeth's hand under his elbow and led her into the house.

Just inside the door, an elderly woman waited. "Good evening, Master Darcy." The woman curtseyed.

Darcy bowed. "Good evening, Mrs. Burns. May I present to you my wife? Mrs. Darcy, this is our housekeeper."

Elizabeth smiled. "I am pleased to meet you."

Mrs. Burns curtseyed, though she eyed Elizabeth with something akin to distrust.

"Though Mrs. Darcy and I are only here for a week, you are to treat her as the mistress of the home. Her primary occupation will be with me, but concerns are to be brought to her, when we are unoccupied with other things. I expect her to be treated with the same respect you and all the staff would give my mother." Darcy spoke firmly, not giving the housekeeper a chance to reply. "I know you will speak to the staff about this and pass along my words."

Mrs. Burns' lips pressed into a flat line, but she replied in the affirmative.

"We would like to warm ourselves. Please direct us to a room with a fire, and bring us a tray of food." Darcy assisted Elizabeth in removing her pelisse, bonnet, and gloves, handing them to Mrs. Burns, along with his greatcoat, hat, and gloves.

"Cook has prepared a nice mutton stew along with freshly baked bread. She has made biscuits for afterwards, I believe."

Darcy nodded. "That sounds delicious." He reached for his wife's hand once more. "In which room has a fire been built?"

"The yellow drawing room, sir."

"Excellent. Bring in our meals as soon as possible, and we will want bathwater when we retire."

"Very good, sir."

Darcy led Elizabeth by the hand, through the back hall to the main one and then up the stairs to a room decorated in soft shades of buttery yellow.

"This is a very nice house." Elizabeth's observation made her husband smile. "We shall have to take a tour tomorrow."

Darcy grinned. "I agree." He drew his wife toward the fireplace, where a merrily flickering blaze radiated heat. Once he had her settled into a chair, he drew its partner closer to hers and settled into it.

The couple remained before the fire, fingers entwined, until the tray containing their meals was brought in. Once they had eaten, they retired to the single room Mrs. Burns had set aside for them, on Mr. George Darcy's orders. They enjoyed a bath, together, and then retired for the night.

Chapter 6

The next day, Darcy and Elizabeth explored the house. Darcy had been there several times over the years, but he found himself fascinated by Elizabeth's reaction. As they went through the rooms, he began recalling stories from his childhood visits and sharing them with her. Often, entrance to a particular room led to kisses and more, so he began to lock the door behind them to keep servants out. Their distraction meant they did not see the entire home, so they continued their tour the following day.

The third morning of their stay, they visited the stables, where Darcy gave Elizabeth a riding lesson before they set out to explore the grounds. They had just come in and refreshed themselves when the housekeeper knocked on the door to their sitting room.

Darcy looked up when he heard the rap on the wood panel. He glanced at the dressing room door and, seeing it standing open, rose from his seat, striding across the room to shut it before calling for the servant to enter.

Mrs. Burns stepped into the room and curtseyed. "If you please, sir, you have visitors. I did not know if you were home?"

Darcy struggled to keep from rolling his eyes. *I am on my honeymoon. Why would I be interested in entertaining?* he thought. To the housekeeper he simply stated. "Who is it?"

"It is Mr. and Mrs. Little from Blackcraig Castle."

Darcy pressed his lips together. "I recall the Littles from my last visit here. Mrs. Darcy and I can spare a quarter hour to visit with them. Put them in the yellow drawing room but do not serve refreshments unless one of us requests them."

With another curtsey, Mrs. Burns stepped back into the hallway, closing the door behind her.

Darcy shook his head as he spun on his heel and approached the dressing room. He knocked, pressing his ear to the door. When Elizabeth bid him enter, he pressed the latch and stepped into the room. He noted with some disappointment that she was seated at the dressing table and wearing a robe.

"I am sorry to disturb you."

A slow smile spread over Elizabeth's countenance. "I am not." She winked.

Darcy flushed, feeling his blood pressure rise at his wife's flirtatiousness. He swallowed, allowing his gaze to wander over her form. Clearing his throat, he brought his eyes back to hers. "Mrs. Burns informs me we have guests."

Elizabeth's smirk fell away as her jaw dropped. "Since when are we expected to entertain the neighbors on our wedding trip?"

Darcy's lips twitched upwards. "My thoughts exactly. I would rather send them on their way, but they are old friends of my parents'. I would hate to disappoint them, and they may well report back to my father." He paused, watching Elizabeth's expression. "It would only be for a quarter hour."

Elizabeth pursed her lips and scowled for a moment. "Very well. I shall be down directly." She focused her gaze on Darcy's eyes. "Only for one quarter hour."

Darcy flashed a grin. "I promise." He laid his hand over his heart as he spoke, then chuckled when Elizabeth rolled her eyes. "I will wait and escort you down. They have arrived unannounced and can very well await our pleasure." He moved toward the table in the corner, intending to sit while he waited.

Elizabeth blinked at her husband for a brief moment, as though surprised that he would remain within her room while she dressed, but then blushed and shrugged. She opened her mouth to speak, but Jenny entered the room at that moment.

"Shall I finish your hair first, Mrs. Darcy?"

"Yes, please do." Elizabeth's lips twisted into a grimace. "Please keep it simple; it seems we have guests and I must dress quickly so Mr. Darcy and I can go greet them." She looked into the mirror at Darcy's reflection. "Is that not so, Mr. Darcy?"

"It is, indeed." Darcy winked at his wife and chuckled when the maid squeaked.

"I am sorry, sir; I did not see you there." Jenny glanced at her mistress with pleading eyes.

"All is well." Elizabeth patted Jenny's arm. "Forgive my husband. He seems to have been infected with a case of mischief this afternoon. Do my hair as quickly as you can so I can dress."

"Yes, ma'am." With quick and efficient movements, Jenny began to brush and then braid Elizabeth's hair. Within a few minutes, she had created an elegant coiffure for her mistress. She turned to the closet. "I chose the green, but perhaps you would prefer a different gown?"

Elizabeth stood from the dressing table, where she had been turning her head back and forth, admiring her hair in the mirror. "I would, yes. The pink, I think. It is newer."

Seconds later, Jenny appeared, the gown draped over her arm. She glanced nervously at Darcy, but resolutely kept her mind focused on her task.

Darcy watched the proceedings carefully. He held his breath when Elizabeth began to slowly untie her robe and slide it off her arms, then let it out in a disappointed sigh when he realized she was completely covered underneath it, with chemise, stays, and petticoats already in place. He shook his head to hear her quiet giggle. "Tease," he muttered.

It did not take long from there for Jenny to get her mistress into the gown and get the tiny buttons in the back done up.

Darcy rose from his seat as Elizabeth approached him. He held his elbow out to her with a smile. "You look very well."

Elizabeth blushed as she took Darcy's arm, but smirked at him. "Thank you, sir."

Darcy chuckled as he led her to the door. Once they reached the corridor, he became silent, as did his wife. They descended the stairs without speaking a word. When they came to the bottom, Elizabeth let go of his arm and he stepped away.

After sharing a look, they made their way to the room where the neighbors waited.

Darcy nodded to the footman to open the door, noting with approval the way Elizabeth lifted her chin before she sailed into the room. He followed, stopping beside her. "Good day." He greeted the Littles with a bow.

"Good day to you, young man. It has been a long time since we have seen you. Will you introduce me to your young lady?" Leighton Little was a broad-shouldered, older gentleman with graying auburn hair and a deep, gravelly voice and blustery manner.

"I will." Darcy turned to his wife. "Please meet Mrs. Elizabeth Darcy. Mrs. Darcy, this is Mr. Leighton Little from Blackcraig Castle. He and his wife are our nearest neighbors here."

Elizabeth curtseyed with a faint smile on her lips. "I am pleased to meet you."

Mr. Little bowed and examined her closely for a long moment. "Likewise." He gestured to his spouse. "This is Mrs. Cora Little, my wife these last five and twenty years or so."

Mrs. Little and Elizabeth exchanged curtseys. "I am happy to make your acquaintance, Mrs. Darcy," the older woman said. "When your Mr. Darcy's father wrote to us that his son had wed and asked us to look in on you, I immediately urged Mr. Little to drive us over here."

Elizabeth's smile remained fixed. "How kind of you. Please, do be seated." She gestured to the grouping of furniture where the Littles had been sitting a few moments before.

As they settled into their seats, Mrs. Little began asking questions. "Tell us about yourself. Mr. George Darcy told us you were from Hertfordshire and not much else. Your father is a gentleman, I assume?"

"Yes, he is. His estate is called Longbourn. I am the second of five daughters."

Mrs. Little pulled back a few inches. "Five daughters? And no sons? Oh, my." She leaned forward again. "What is your age? You appear full young to be a wife."

Elizabeth clenched her jaw for a moment but then swallowed and replied. "I am just past my seventeenth birthday."

Mrs. Little's hand rose to rest on her chest. "Oh, you are young! How long have you been out in society? How did you meet your husband?"

"My mother put my sisters and me out when we reached fifteen. My eldest sister has been out for two years and my next younger will make her debut in two or three months." Elizabeth's spine stiffened. She was beginning to flush; she could feel the heat rising up her neck. "My marriage to Mr. Darcy was arranged. I met him the day I married him."

Darcy, seeing the clues indicating his wife's anger, stepped in to turn the conversation in another direction. "The weather here has been very fine. Mrs. Darcy and I have enjoyed several outings in the last couple of days."

"Ah, yes. We are in the midst of a delightful spring season. I cannot recall one finer." Mr. Little took up his part in the conversation and a brief discussion followed of the Darcys' activities and Elizabeth's impressions of the area. Mrs. Little was apparently on a mission, though, because it was not long before she asked another intrusive question.

"Do you play, Mrs. Darcy?"

"A little and very poorly." Elizabeth softened her comment with a slight lifting of the corners of her lips. "I am afraid I could not trouble myself to practice, and when my younger sister took an interest in it, time at the instrument became difficult to find."

Mrs. Little's brows rose to her hairline at this response. The remainder of the visit was filled with questions that became increasingly invasive into the young couple's privacy.

The final straw for Elizabeth came when her female visitor asked, in front of the gentlemen, if she had any questions about doing her wifely duty.

Mrs. Little leaned forward and lowered her voice as her husband and Darcy exchanged remarks about the hunting in the area. "I daresay you have questions and concerns about what happens in the bedroom." Her smile remained friendly and her eyes calculating, as they had all during the visit. "Mr. George Darcy has often relayed to us the recalcitrant behavior of his son. If Fitzwilliam Darcy has hurt you, I would be happy to give you advice, since your mother is not near."

"Thank you, madam, but my mother gave me a thorough set of instructions when I married. I am well aware of my duty and how it all is supposed to work. Nothing my husband has done is any different than what she explained would happen." Elizabeth breathed in through her nose and stood. "Thank you for your concern."

When Elizabeth rose, Darcy and the Littles did, as well.

"Oh, dear. I hope I did not offend you." Mrs. Little reached over and patted her hostess' hand.

Elizabeth dipped her head and managed to speak without clenching her jaw. "All is well." She tipped her lips up again into the small smile that had earlier been fixed to her face.

"Did you invite the lass to dine, Mrs. Little?"

"Oh! I forgot!" The older woman turned to Elizabeth. "Mr. George Darcy informs us that you are leaving the area Thursday next. We should like to invite you to dine with us on Wednesday." Mrs. Little clasped her hands together. "It will be the four of us and two or three other couples. The neighbors shall all be eager to meet you, you know."

Elizabeth pressed her lips into a line as she turned to look at her husband. "I would not mind it, but I shall defer to Mr. Darcy."

"We should be delighted. Thank you for extending the invitation." Darcy bowed shallowly.

"Excellent." Mr. Little's voice boomed. "We keep country hours; we shall expect you at six o'clock on Wednesday."

The Littles said their good-byes at this point, and the Darcys escorted them to the door. The moment the portal closed behind the older couple, Darcy turned himself and his wife around and, with his hand on the small of her back, guided her into the drawing room. He shut and locked the door behind them, led Elizabeth down the room to the second door, and shut and locked it, as well. Then, he took her hand and pulled her to the far side of the fireplace, out of sight of the windows. There, he wrapped his arms around her and held her close. He bent his head and kissed her hair. "I am so sorry. I tried to steer the conversation in other directions but the lady was ruthless."

Elizabeth, upon being pulled into her husband's arms, immediately wrapped hers around his waist and buried her face in his chest. "She was horrible. Her last question was far beyond the pale. I could perhaps forgive her if she had inquired about such a topic when you and her husband were on the far side of the room, or even in another part of the house, but to ask about what goes on in our private chambers where anyone could hear was too much!" She pulled her head away from Darcy's body and looked up at him. "The longer I think about it, the angrier I get. And I sat there, knowing that she was going to report every word we said to your despicable father. You know by now, I hope, that I find you very likeable and I do not at all mean by what I am about to say that I regret you. I do not. This situation could have been so much worse for me, but … I am so angry with it all. Why could we not have courted so I could choose on my own? Why does your father have to be so vulgar and disgusting? I hate having to be someone I am not for the neighbors and the servants."

Darcy tightened his arms around Elizabeth's stiff form as her voice began to rise. "Shh. I know; I feel the same." He ran a hand up and down her spine. "I have lived this way for so long that I cannot imagine living free from fear."

"That is so sad. You are so different from your father. I suppose you could change, after all, we have only been married ten or eleven days, but I somehow do not believe you will."

Darcy looked Elizabeth in the eye. "I have worked hard my entire life to be different than my father. I have sought out better models of gentlemanly behavior and tried to emulate them. I have no wish to follow the same path he took." He pressed Elizabeth's head back into his chest and squeezed her close. "I wish I could change things for you." He kissed her head again, his hand cradling it. Then, he moved it down to wrap around her shoulder and lowered his head. He whispered, "I am sorry." When she looked at him, he kissed her softly once, then again.

A few minutes later, after they were both breathless, the couple separated.

"Shall we take a walk?" Darcy looked outside. "The sun is shining again. We could ask the cook for a basket and picnic on the riverbank."

"I like that idea." Elizabeth wiped her eyes and moved to look out the window as Darcy unlocked the doors, then rang for a servant.

Darcy returned to his wife's side after making his request of the housekeeper. He stood behind her, his hands on her hips. "It will not be long, I do not think. Shall we wait in the entry hall?"

Elizabeth turned. "Yes, let us do that." She smiled a little and ducked her head, lifting a hand to run down his damp waistcoat. "I am sorry for crying all over you. I hope it is not ruined."

Darcy shrugged as he examined the wet spots. "I doubt it. Smith is very good at saving my clothing from stains, and if he cannot, I will simply order another."

Elizabeth shook her head. "Very well, then. Shall we go?"

With a wink and a smirk, Darcy tilted his head and held out his elbow. "We shall." He escorted Elizabeth to the room's entrance and, seeing no one in the hall, led her to the front door. A maid appeared with their hats and gloves. They had no more than donned the items when the basket from the kitchen appeared. Thus equipped, the pair exited the house and began to wander along the path to the river. As they had earlier, they were silent, each contemplating their situation, the incidents of the morning, and what they may face when they reached Pemberley.

Chapter 7

Once they had chosen a pretty spot under a tree to spread out the blanket Darcy brought, and had eaten the majority of the meat, cheese, and bread from the basket, they leaned back against the trunk to watch the numerous ducks floating by on the water and the fish jumping out of it. After a long period of quiet, Elizabeth asked her husband a question.

"Why? Why is your father doing this? I know what mine told me, but I do not understand yours."

Darcy had wrapped his arm around Elizabeth's shoulder as they had settled into their place, and now ran his hand up and down her arm. He sighed. "I am not certain why he has done this. I suspect he had debts but have not worked out how it relates to you and your family."

Elizabeth shook her head. "I do not know. Were our fathers acquainted somehow?"

Darcy shrugged. "I have never heard of any Bennets coming around, but I was at school much of the time."

Elizabeth thought a while. "My uncle in town, Uncle Gardiner, lends people money. His main occupation is selling goods from the Far

East, but often, people bring him items in exchange for cash. If they do not pay him back, he sells their things. I wonder if that is the connection. It would make sense, given what my father told me."

Darcy looked from the river to his wife. "Which was?"

"Just what I said before, that Mama became very ill with nerves at some point, and they thought she would die, because of the entail. She needed the assurance that one of us would marry well so she would be saved. Jane was not chosen because she is so beautiful and Mama wishes for her to marry high, so I was sacrificed. Uncle Gardiner is Mama's brother."

Darcy nodded. "I remember overhearing my father and the earl speaking about my sister's dowry. It is tied up in my mother's settlement in such a way that Father cannot touch it. My uncle was quite adamant that my father find a solution to his problems that did not involve dishonoring my mother's family and ruining her childrens' prospects. I wager he went to your uncle for a loan and instead of accepting items as security, Mr. Gardiner insisted on a marriage."

Elizabeth sighed. "You are probably right." She looked down. "It does not make me feel better."

"I am sorry." Darcy squeezed her shoulder and kissed her hair. "If I were of age, things might be different." He leaned his head on hers.

Elizabeth slipped her arm around her husband's back. "What happens if I do not get with child within the time frame he expects?"

"I lose the rest of my inheritance, and access to my sister. She will have no one to defend and protect her and will be vulnerable to his mean temper and disgusting, tawdry schemes." Darcy lifted his head. "I cannot allow that to happen. She is only eight years old. She is a baby still."

Elizabeth squeezed Darcy's waist. "It will not happen. We have been diligent in trying, and my mother had Jane barely a year after my parents married. If I am anything like her, I will follow suit. If the unthinkable happens and I do not fall pregnant in time, we will have to come up with some way to take care of Georgiana."

"You have such a kind heart." Darcy tilted Elizabeth's face up with his finger under her chin. "If my father knew that ahead of time, I doubt he would have agreed to our marriage." A corner of his lips lifted and fell in a moment. His gaze roamed her face, settling on her eyes, so close to his. "Thank you." He kissed her softly.

Hours later, as the sun began to dip low in the sky, Darcy and Elizabeth rose from their picnic spot and made the trek back to the house. They held hands and chattered about anything and everything.

<div align="center">~~~***~~~</div>

The next days passed quickly. Darcy and Elizabeth spent nearly every waking hour together in some pursuit or other. They became close, isolated as they were. Darcy had given orders to Mrs. Burns that no other visitors were to be admitted. It was risky, doing such a thing, because he knew his father would, at the least, have a scathing comment about it. Despite the risks, Darcy found himself wanting more and more time alone with his wife. She fascinated him. Never before had he met a girl who challenged him as she did. She questioned him on everything and refused to blindly follow his every directive. She bested him at chess and backgammon, and skillfully negated his every opinion in a debate. Best of all, she did all of this in such an arch manner that he could not be angry. He felt himself falling further and further under her spell. For the first time in a long time, he felt happy and fulfilled.

Elizabeth did not know how Darcy felt about her. They did not speak of feelings at all, and she could not discern them from his manner. He sometimes appeared all haughtiness and arrogance, but then he would laugh or smirk and spoil the effect.

For her part, Elizabeth was drawn to her husband in ways she did not understand. She noticed the care he took with her whenever they were alone, and she appreciated that he asked her opinion on things and instructed Mrs. Burns about visitors. He never spoke down to her, as some of the gentlemen in Meryton used to. He never made fun of her or laughed at her, as her father was wont to do. He made her feel special and beautiful, and she loved that. I could easily fall in love with him, she thought.

On their second to the last day in Scotland, Darcy and Elizabeth strolled up the river to the edge of the estate. They held hands and stopped frequently to share kisses, knowing no one would see them. They reached the low stone wall that separated Glenmoor from the neighboring estate and began to walk along it when they heard a tiny mewl.

"Did you hear that?" Elizabeth stopped, holding her hand up to keep Darcy from speaking. She cocked her head to listen and soon, she heard the sound again. She looked at her husband.

Darcy's brow creased. "That sounds like a kitten."

"That is what I thought, as well." She began looking around for the creature. Darcy joined her and it was not long before they found the tiny thing, all alone, stuck in a crevice between two stones.

"Oh," Elizabeth cried. "It could die in there! We must save it!"

Darcy found he could not deny her, and so between the two of them, and after he had re-moved his tailcoat and carefully draped it over the fence so Elizabeth's gown would not be-come dirty when she leaned over it, they man-aged to pull the sometimes-spitting ball of fur out of the spot into which it had been wedged.

Elizabeth cuddled the kitten to her neck. It had calmed immediately upon being lifted out of its hole and was now purring and rubbing its face on her. "It is so adorable!"

"It is that." Darcy rubbed his finger over the cat's fur. "We cannot keep it, though. I shudder to think what my father would do to it, likely in front of us."

Elizabeth seemed to deflate for a moment. "Oh." She sighed. "I should have known. Is there someone we can give it to who will care for it?"

"Perhaps. We can at least try." Darcy thought a moment. "Let us request the carriage. We can ride into town and see if we can find someone there to take it."

"Thank you." Elizabeth's eyes shone. "You are a good man, Fitzwilliam Darcy."

"Thank you." Darcy felt the arrow of his wife's admiration hit him in the heart. He stood tall and proud the rest of the day. I could fall in love with her very easily. Maybe I already have, he thought.

The final day of their stay at Glenmoor House finally arrived. The morning was spent riding about the estate, saying a silent goodbye to the beautiful landscape and the now-familiar paths. They had tea in their rooms and worked on becoming parents. Then, they bathed and dressed and drove to Blackcraig for dinner with the Littles.

In addition to their hosts, there were three couples from the neighborhood: the Bruces, the Turners, and the Lewises. Mrs. Little maintained the barely concealed haughtiness that she had first displayed at Glenmoor House. Elizabeth maintained a superficial politeness that perfectly matched that of her hostess.

As for the other ladies in the group, they were all older than Elizabeth. Scarlett Bruce was a white-haired grandmother with a forthrightness that bordered on rude. Nina Turner and Fern Lewis were about the age of Cora Little. They had children who were mostly grown. None had anything in common with Elizabeth beyond being female. After an initial but blessedly brief interrogation once the ladies had separated from the gentlemen, they left her largely to her own devices.

A quarter hour after separating, the gentlemen joined their wives.

"We must have some music." Mrs. Little's declaration was met with applause. "Mrs. Darcy, you must play for us. We have all heard each other often enough. It will be nice to hear someone new."

Though she wished to refuse, Elizabeth assented with as much grace as she could muster. When her husband offered to turn pages for her, she accepted, thanking him quietly once they were seated at the instrument.

"I could see you did not wish to exhibit. I could not leave you alone to do something you had no desire to." Darcy accepted the sheets of music his wife handed him.

"I do not wish to." Elizabeth sorted through the pieces on the pianoforte, finally settling on one that she remembered playing before but had never mastered. "I only hope I do not embarrass you."

"You could not do so, Elizabeth. Do your best, and I will get us out of here as quickly as I can."

With a nod, Elizabeth arranged the sheets and began to play. She fudged and slurred her way through much of it, but when she was finished, felt that she had done a creditable job. She then began to play a piece she had memorized and knew she performed well. She sang along with this one and was gratified at the enthusiastic reception her effort received.

Darcy escorted Elizabeth back to the sofa, helping her sit and then taking a place beside her. Mrs. Lewis took over at the pianoforte, and conversation swirled along with the after-dinner tea. True to his word, Darcy extricated himself and his wife from the event as soon as he could. As he sat beside her in the dark carriage, he reflected on her song. *She adds emotion to it that makes up for her lack of technical proficiency,* he thought. *I could listen to her all day.* He lifted her hand, which he had grasped upon sitting, and kissed it. She is perfect.

The couple rose early the next morning, while it was still dark. Darcy was dressed, except for his tailcoat, and was in the bedroom, waiting on Elizabeth. Hearing a knock on the door, he called out for the person to enter.

"Forgive me for disturbing you, sir." Smith entered and bowed.

Darcy stood in the middle of the room. He could tell from his valet's demeanor that something was not as expected. "What has happened?"

Smith cleared his throat. "I went down to check the carriage set aside for me and Jenny. When I arrived at the drive, there was only one. Mr. Drover informed me that Mr. George Darcy had directed him in a note he received yesterday to only prepare one vehicle."

Darcy rolled his eyes. "Lovely." He paused as he allowed this news to filter through his mind. "You know this means he will probably have botched the arrangements for the inns, as well. He takes great delight in making us squirm."

"That he does, and I suspect you are correct." Smith gestured toward the dressing room. "Jenny and I will be able to ride up top with the driver for at least a little while each day, as long as the weather stays fine. I am certain she will not mind, and you know I do not."

"No, I know that." Darcy sighed. "I should have known we would not get away from Scotland without something being done."

"I am sorry, sir." Smith's tone was full of regret.

"Thank you, but it is not your fault. I am not certain it is even mine. I have behaved almost exactly as he would have expected me to, except for charging Mrs. Burns to turn away guests." Darcy glanced at the dressing room door when he heard Elizabeth's voice. "I will make Mrs. Darcy aware of the situation. I am certain she will insist you ride inside, but I would like some time alone with her, so I plan to override her for a couple hours, at least."

"Very good, sir. If you have no further need of me, I will finish packing your trunks and get them down to the carriage. It will be tight with four adults and all that luggage, but we will manage." Smith quieted, waiting for his master's instructions.

"That is all. I appreciate the warning." Darcy dismissed the valet and sighed, turning towards the window. He leaned against the frame, considering what the carriage situation meant and dreading what was likely to come. He felt tense for the first time since arriving at Glenmoor House.

"William?" Elizabeth walked up behind her husband and peeked around him to see the sun beginning its rise over the horizon. "Are we ready?"

"Mostly." Darcy turned around and pulled Elizabeth into his arms for a kiss. "Mmmm, I needed that," he said when he finally released her lips.

"What is the matter?" Elizabeth's eyes roamed Darcy's features. "You are stiff as a board and that is not like you."

Darcy sighed. "My father has struck."

Elizabeth's brows creased. "What do you mean? Has he arrived here?"

"No, no." Darcy paused. "My father does not allow me to make my own travel arrangements. He prefers to be in control of every aspect of everyone's life, as much as he can manage it. In the usual course of things, we would have two carriages as we travel: an older one for Smith and Jenny and the luggage, and a newer one for us. When Smith went down this morning to check the older carriage and supervise the loading of trunks, the coachman informed him that my father ordered just one equipage for this trip, which means ..."

"We will be all squished together for three days in one coach, with our luggage in our laps." Elizabeth shook her head.

"Yes, that is it in a nutshell." Darcy ran his finger along Elizabeth's cheek. "Smith has offered to ride with the driver for part of the day and will ask your maid to do the same." When Elizabeth took a breath and opened her mouth to speak, Darcy laid his finger over her lips, stopping her words before they started. "I wish for them to do so, at least for part of the day, as long as the weather remains nice. I have plans for you that I do not wish to put off."

Elizabeth's brow rose. "Plans? What kind of plans?"

Darcy grinned and pulled her closer, wrapping his arms around her and leaning down to whisper in her ear. He chuckled when she instantly blushed beet red and buried her face in his chest. He kissed her ear and then let go of her, grasping her hand. "I will not if you object. I would do nothing that you are not completely comfortable with."

Elizabeth could barely look Darcy in the face. "Well, kissing I do not mind. I know that already. As for the rest ... I do not know."

Darcy lifted her hand and kissed it. "Very well. We shall see what happens." He tucked it under his elbow. "Are you ready to go down? I am certain the carriage will be prepared by now. We will break our fast when we make the first exchange of horses, unless you require something before we leave."

"I am ready, and no, I need nothing now. Jenny brought me up a pot of tea; that should last me for a couple hours."

Chapter 8

Hours later, Darcy stood in the center of a tiny room at the top floor of the inn his father had sent them to. He turned to the innkeeper. "Are you quite certain Mr. George Darcy reserved this particular room for us? For his son and daughter-in-law?"

The proprietor lifted his chin. "I am. He instructed that I go to no extra expense to host you, and made it clear that your servants could sleep with you."

"I see." Darcy swallowed down a rush of anger. After a long and uncomfortable day cooped up in a cramped carriage in need of new springs, he had been looking forward to cuddling his wife in a comfortable bed. The one in this room looked thin and lumpy, from what he could see. There was barely room to move around. "Very well. Thank you for your consideration." He watched as the owner bowed and scurried from the room.

Elizabeth looked at Darcy. "What will we do?"

"If it were just me and Smith, we would share the bed." Darcy sighed to himself. "It is not Smith and me, though. I would rather not share my bed with my valet when I could do so with my wife." He startled when Elizabeth giggled at his words.

"I am sorry." She rushed to reassure him. "It was not what you said that amused me, it was how you said it." Elizabeth stepped toward him and wrapped her arms around his waist, heedless of their servants standing near the window.

Darcy returned Elizabeth's embrace. "We cannot have Jenny sleeping downstairs. I know other women have done it, but it is dangerous."

"I agree. The only solution we really have is for all of us to sleep in this room." Elizabeth stepped back, letting Darcy go. She turned to her maid. "What is your opinion, Jenny?"

"If the innkeep will give us extra bedding, we can make pallets on the floor and Smith and I can sleep there."

Darcy's training as a gentleman fought with his selfish desire to sleep beside his wife. He was already weary. A night on the hard floor would not lead to rest. However, he could not allow a female, no matter her station, to do it, either. "I agree except on one point. I propose the ladies take the bed. Smith and I will sleep on the floor."

Elizabeth hesitated but agreed. "I suppose that would be best." She turned to her maid. "You do not snore, do you?" She winked.

Jenny giggled. "No, ma'am, I do not believe I do. The gentlemen very well may, however."

Darcy and Smith both sniffed, making the ladies laugh.

"I am a Darcy. I do not snore." Darcy's declaration led to more teases from his wife. They drew a tired smile to his face.

Two hours later, after a meal in the taproom and the delivery of extra bedding by a maid, the Darcys and their servants laid down in their respective beds. The ladies fell asleep rather quickly. Smith was not far behind them. Darcy, however, tossed and turned. He was supremely uncomfortable on the floor. Combined with the fear and anger that had his stomach tied into a knot, he found it impossible to fall asleep. He lay for hours creating scenarios in his mind where he finally stood up to his father and came out the winner.

~~~***~~~

The next day was a tense one for the entire party. Having remained awake until nearly dawn, Darcy was cantankerous. His ill humor left everyone on edge, including Elizabeth and Jenny, who had slept reasonably well. The servants elected to ride above for the first leg or two of the trip, despite the damp chill of the early morning.
~~~

With the other side of the equipage empty, Elizabeth urged her husband to stretch out. When he did so, she wedged herself into the corner and had him lie back, using her for a pillow. She read aloud to him for a short while and soon, he was sound asleep. He rested in that manner for four hours, sleeping through the first change of horses. Smith and Jenny retrieved pastries and cider in a basket so Elizabeth could break her fast, and Darcy, as well, once he had awakened.

The nap went a long way to restoring Darcy's mood, though he remained resentful. He was also worried. "Not knowing what is ahead is unpleasant," he said to Elizabeth during one of their stops. "He has been known to arrange for me to sleep in a barn. One would think he would not do something like that to you, but look what he has arranged so far. I cannot abide the thought of what he might put you through simply to make me look bad."

"I would never blame you for the situations we find ourselves in here." Elizabeth did her best to assure Darcy that she held him blameless. "He ought to allow you to make the arrangements. I cannot imagine someone being so ungenerous and malicious with his own child. I am sorry he is doing this, if only because it is causing you pain."

Darcy lifted Elizabeth's hand off his arm where it rested, and kissed it. "You are too good. I am happy that if I must go through this, it is with you." He kissed her hand again, longing to hold her in his arms and kiss her lips. He looked around at the busy courtyard and sighed.

Elizabeth smiled, looking pleased that she had cheered him. "Tell me of Pemberley."

Darcy handed her up into the coach. "You will be happier there, I think, than at Glenmoor." He followed her in, and spoke of the Derbyshire estate while they waited for Smith and Jenny. "The servants are different at Pemberley. There are plenty who will run to my father with tales, but there are many who will not. Mrs. Reynolds is the housekeeper." Darcy went on to explain that Mrs. Reynolds had been with the family since he was four years old and that she was often stuck in the middle between George Darcy and his children.

Elizabeth nodded her understanding. "I would hate to be in her position. You say she ignores many of your father's directives?"

"Yes, if she feels it will harm myself or my sister, she ignores it. My father would never dare fire her; she is aware of everything that has happened at Pemberley since the day she was hired. She promised my mother to watch over us, and she has kept that promise, even to the point of threatening to tell of my father's misdeeds all over England. That does not stop him from abusing her, but it does guarantee her a permanent position."

"I would say so. Do you think I will like her? Will she like me?"

"She will love you, because you make me happy." Darcy looked across the carriage to his valet. "Do you not agree, Smith?"

Smith looked from the window to the master. "I do. Mrs. Reynolds loves you and Miss Darcy like you were her own children. She will love anyone who makes you smile and laugh the way Mrs. Darcy does."

Darcy grinned and turned to his wife. "There. You see?"

Elizabeth smiled. "I do. I am happy to hear it."

The remainder of the day passed in a similar manner, with Darcy giving his wife a lecture on life at Pemberley and Elizabeth sharing stories about her childhood.

Darcy's improved frame of mind lasted until they stopped for the night. While the room was larger than the one from the previous night, there still had been no provision made for the servants. There was no sitting room attached, either, which is something he was accustomed to having. One would have provided a perfectly adequate room for Jenny, and Smith would have been able to sleep in the taproom. To make matters worse, no extra bedding could be had. The inn was full up and every spare blanket and sheet had already been spoken for.

Darcy did his best to hold in his growing anger. It would not do to take it out on those it was his duty to protect. He had been serious when he told Elizabeth that he did everything with an eye to behaving differently than his father. He would not begin now to do differently and risk destroying his blossoming relationship. So, he swallowed down his complaints and thoughts and made the best of it.

The following morning was rainy, and the servants rode inside the carriage with Darcy and Elizabeth. Though they were cramped together and even Elizabeth was becoming short-tempered, the four attempted to rest as much as possible.

The inn they stopped at this third night was a mere half-day's ride from Pemberley. Darcy would have liked to push on, but had learned long ago to obey his father's directives or face the consequences. One never knew what kind of mood the elder Darcy would be in, or his state of inebriation. To cross him often meant a brow-beating or worse. The son learned early not to rile his father unnecessarily. Though George Darcy was not supposed to be at Pemberley at this point in time, it did not mean he had not taken it into his head to travel there and asses his son's progress himself. So, the group stopped at the Sceptre and Anvil.

To Darcy's surprise, better accommodations had been made at this inn. The room was tiny, with just enough room for a bed and a chest of drawers. There was a miniscule sitting room attached containing two wingback chairs and a fireplace.

Elizabeth could clearly see that though her husband was pleased to be able to sleep with her instead of on the floor, he was not happy with the quality of the rooms. She could tell without looking that the mattress was thin and lumpy, and barely wide enough to accommodate two adults. She heard Darcy grumble under his breath as he surveyed the space. Though she was just as tired as he appeared to be, she strove to hold her tongue and make the best of the situation. "Jenny," she asked, "will you be able to rest in the sitting room?"

"Yes, ma'am. I can pull the chairs close to each other, face to face, and stretch my legs out. I will be quite comfortable." Jenny's words were decisive.

Elizabeth tipped her head. "Good." She turned to Smith. "You will sleep in the public room, then? You do not mind?"

Smith bowed. "I do not mind at all. The raucousness will begin to diminish in an hour or two and I will claim a table top or bench for my own. It will be far more comfortable than the floor, I assure you."

Elizabeth chuckled. "I would imagine so." She turned to Darcy. "And, you, sir?"

"I am sleeping with you." Darcy slid a look at the small bed. "Though, it may be a tight fit."

With a smile, Elizabeth followed his gaze. "I suspected you might. Do you have any objections to Jenny and Smith sleeping as they have suggested?"

Darcy shook his head. "No. The sitting room is the only part of this scenario that pleases me more than a private room with my wife. I am sorry, Smith, that you must sleep downstairs, but it is an improvement over the stables."

Smith laughed. "That it is. I would ask if you and Mrs. Darcy would like a bath." He looked around. "But the room is too small to fit a tub. I shall bring up a ewer or two of hot water. Will that do?"

"It will, yes. Given the level of noise coming from the taproom, I think we should eat up here." Darcy turned to Elizabeth. "Do you agree?"

Elizabeth shrugged. "I do not mind sitting with the rabble; I would imagine it would be highly diverting. However, I suspect you are not of a mind to be amused in such a manner, so I will agree."

"Thank you." Darcy turned to Smith. "Order four meals brought up. You and Jenny may eat with us." He began to turn toward the bed. "Thank heavens I am allowed this much autonomy, else I should go mad."

With a sympathetic look at his master, Smith bowed and exited the room. Jenny occupied herself with changing the sheets on the bed and laying out nightclothes for Elizabeth.

"There is not even privacy for using the chamber pot." Darcy's disgusted grumble made his wife frown at him.

"You are right." Elizabeth sighed. "We shall have to turn our backs on each other or go out back to the privy."

"I do not want you going outside alone past that group of drunken farmers to use the outhouse." Darcy raised his voice just enough to assure his wife of his anger.

Though she would have liked to argue, the fact was that Elizabeth was not happy at the thought of walking around in the dark in a strange place. "I will not. It was only a suggestion." She glanced at Jenny, noting the way the maid kept her eyes on her task.

Darcy must have noticed her concern, because when he spoke again, he moderated his voice. "I know. I am sorry." He ran his hand through his hair and backed away to give Jenny room, bumping the dresser behind him.

Elizabeth said nothing, merely nodding her acceptance of his apology. She squeezed herself into a corner as the maid finished up. Within a few minutes, Smith was back, followed by another maid carrying a tray. The four arranged themselves on the bed and floor and enjoyed the hearty meal of chicken pie. Once they were finished eating, they readied themselves for sleep.

Darcy and Elizabeth arranged themselves in the tiny bed as best they could. After trying a couple different positions, they found they fit best when Elizabeth was on her side with Darcy at her back. He wrapped her in his arms, her back to his chest, and sighed. "I have missed this." He kissed her ear.

Elizabeth smiled. "I have, as well." She cringed when the noise level from below suddenly rose. "I hope it helps us sleep better."

In the end, her hope was for naught. Between the noises of the revelers below, the sounds of beds creaking and couples moaning in the rooms surrounding them, and the discomfort of the bed she and Darcy were in, neither Elizabeth nor her husband slept very much. When Smith knocked on the door at dawn, they groaned in unison.

Chapter 9

Despite their lack of rest, it did not take the Darcys long to rise and dress. A maid brought them tea and scones, and soon, they were walking out of the inn and ascending into the coach.

Darcy had said not a word, which had suited Elizabeth just fine. After three days of travel with an unhappy gentleman and a night of little sleep, she was grateful for the silence. About mid-day, the carriage slowed, turning in at a set of gates. She noticed her husband perk up. They travelled down a long drive which made a turn. She was surprised when the equipage stopped and Darcy hopped out.

"Come," he said, holding his hand out for Elizabeth to take. With a puzzled look, she placed her palm in his and allowed him to assist her to the ground.

"I arranged with the coachman to have the carriage stop here on the ridge, so you could see the house at its best advantage." Darcy turned his wife around.

Upon seeing the large, stone structure, Elizabeth's hands flew to her mouth. "Oh, my!" Her eyes darted to and fro, examining the huge house. She turned to Darcy. "It is beautiful! Can we not live here forever?"

Darcy chuckled. "We will spend as much time here as we can. I much prefer Pemberley to anywhere else."

Elizabeth turned again. "Oh, I hope we can be here most of the year, at least." She gripped Darcy's hand. "I can see this view covered in snow at Christmastide." She leaned back and into her husband's arms for a moment.

Darcy smiled, hugging Elizabeth close and kissing her. "It is beautiful covered in snow. You like it then?"

"Well, I have not seen the inside, but if it is half as beautiful as the outside, I will love it!"

Darcy looked into his wife's sparkling eyes and warm smile and, forgetting his anger and resentment, felt his heart skip a beat. He leaned his head forward, and as his lips captured hers, his eyes slid shut. The couple kissed slow and deep for a long moment. The stamping of the horses' hooves soon reminded them of their location. Blushing, they climbed back up into the equipage and the carriage carried them down the drive.

A short time later, they stopped again, this time at the side of the house. Again, Darcy descended first, assisting Elizabeth. He tucked her arm under his and led her through a dark hallway and into a large courtyard. Along the walls were several doors and windows on each side. In the center was a bubbling fountain that lent a sense of calm to those who passed by. They entered the house, stepping into another long and dark but wider corridor which led to a large, bright, and airy entry hall. There to greet them was an older lady, who immediately curtsied.

"Welcome home, Master Darcy."

"Thank you; I am happy to be home." Darcy removed his hat and gloves and handed them to a waiting maid. "Allow me to introduce my wife to you." He turned to Elizabeth. "This is Mrs. Elizabeth Darcy. Mrs. Darcy, this is Pemberley's housekeeper, Mrs. Reynolds."

Elizabeth smiled at the older woman. "I am pleased to make your acquaintance."

Mrs. Reynolds curtseyed. "I am happy to meet you." She glanced at Darcy. "If you require anything, please do tell me."

"All I need at the moment is a hot bath and a meal. I am afraid our journey was long and not particularly comfortable." Elizabeth looked up at Darcy. "Would you agree?"

"Indeed I do." Darcy's lips lifted a little at the corners as he spoke to his wife, then fell when he addressed the housekeeper. "I am taking Mrs.

Darcy to the schoolroom to meet my sister first, unless there is some reason I should not?"

Mrs. Reynolds shook her head. "No, sir, there is nothing special going on that I am aware of. Miss Robinson has said nothing to me. I am certain Miss Darcy will welcome the interruption."

"Then, we will go up now. Send someone to alert us when our baths are ready. The trays of food should be sent up a half hour following." Darcy extended his elbow toward Elizabeth. When she tucked her hand around it, he began walking toward the staircase.

Elizabeth looked around in awe at the massive entry hall with its ceiling painted with clouds and angels, and its lavishly decorated walls. "What a beautiful room." She turned to Darcy. "It is clearly expensively done but is not off-putting in the least. I would not call it warm, but it seems to invite one in."

Darcy smiled a little at Elizabeth's words. "My mother took great pride in making Pemberley a home. She would be pleased by your sentiments, if she could hear them." He glanced around at the familiar space as he took to the stairs. "Her sister, Lady Catherine, has decorated her home just as lavishly, but in an overbearing way that reminds one just what her standing is." He shuddered. "I much prefer Pemberley to Rosings."

Elizabeth squeezed Darcy's arm. "I can see why. It is beautiful. You will have to give me a tour." They reached the next floor and turned to climb up another set of steps. "The place is so large, I fear getting lost." She laughed lightly.

Darcy chuckled. "I will do that, but do not fear getting lost. There is usually a servant or two around, even in the unused parts of the building, and if there is not, every room has a bell pull. Someone will come find you."

Elizabeth smiled but said nothing as they reached the top step. She followed Darcy's lead as he guided her to the next set of stairs and up into a large, airy, open space. At a table near a window sat a young girl with long, blonde hair and an older woman in a grey gown. The eyes of both were drawn to the doorway as Elizabeth and Darcy entered. The little girl jumped up and ran toward them. Elizabeth watched as Darcy moved a step away and braced himself.

"Brother! You have come home!" Georgiana threw herself into Darcy's arms.

Darcy lifted his sister up and swung her around. "I have! Did you miss me?" He stopped moving and hugged her. "Are you well?"

The small blonde leaned back in her brother's arms and placed her hands on either side of his face. "I am now." She smiled for a moment, but it faltered when she heard the footsteps of her governess approaching.

Darcy noticed his sister's altered demeanor and whispered to her. "We will talk later." When she nodded, he set her on the floor. He threw a stern look at the governess, who had opened her mouth to speak, then looked back at Georgiana. "I brought someone with me. Would you consent to meet her?"

Georgiana looked at Elizabeth, who was smiling at the sight of the siblings' reunion, and recalled a recent lesson on etiquette. "Yes, please do introduce us, Brother."

"Do you remember that I told you Father arranged a marriage for me?" When his sister nodded, Darcy continued. "I went away to marry and go on a wedding trip. This is my wife, Mrs. Elizabeth Darcy." He turned to Elizabeth. "Mrs. Darcy, please meet my sister, Miss Georgiana Darcy." He watched as the two curtsied to each other.

"I am happy to meet you, Miss Darcy." Elizabeth smiled, delighted with the polite and apparently loving behavior of her new sister. "I had to leave my four sisters behind at Longbourn, and I dearly hope you and I can be friends."

Georgiana's eyes widened. "You have four sisters?" She turned her gaze to her brother. "I only have Fitzwilliam. I cannot imagine having one sister, much less four. How old are they? Do they have lessons like I do? What are their names?"

Elizabeth grinned. "One is older and three are younger. Jane is older. She is nine and ten. Mary is five and ten, Catherine is three and ten, and Lydia is one and ten."

"Oh, I am eight. Miss Lydia is not much older than me." Georgiana clasped her hands in front of her chest.

"She is not." Elizabeth leaned forward and lowered her voice. "If I am honest, she is spoiled and often behaves much younger than her age."

Georgiana's eyes widened again. She fell silent, as though she did not know how to respond to such information.

A knock on the doorframe behind them made the four turn as one toward the door. Smith stood there, eyes cast down. When Darcy bid him to speak, he informed them that baths were waiting in their dressing rooms.

"Thank you. We shall be down directly." Darcy turned back to Georgiana. "We will come back up this evening and tuck you into bed.

Then, I will take you riding tomorrow. How does that sound?"

"It sounds wonderful! Thank you!" Georgiana hugged her brother tightly around the waist, then reached for Elizabeth, granting her new sister the same affection.

"Come, Miss Darcy. You must allow your brother and his wife," she sneered at the word, "to go. They did not bother to clean up from the road before they visited." Miss Robinson started to turn Georgiana back toward the table.

Darcy glared at the governess, the anger at his situation, which he had kept under good regulation in front of his sister, displaying itself in the daggers that came out of his eyes. "Remember your place, madam. You will treat Mrs. Darcy as the mistress of Pemberley, for that is what she is as the eldest Darcy female in residence."

Miss Robinson had stilled when Darcy spoke to her. Her eyes narrowed on his face and her jaw visibly clenched, but she did not reply to him. Instead, she curtseyed silently and led Georgiana away.

Darcy stared after the governess, a muscle in his jaw ticking. Anger rolled off him in waves, and Elizabeth remained silent, glancing between her husband and the retreating servant. She lifted her hand, placing it on Darcy's and causing him to startle.

"I am sorry. Come; let us go to our rooms." Darcy turned and gestured for Elizabeth to precede him out the door, where Smith waited.

"I apologize for interrupting, sir."

"It was nothing. I asked someone to inform me and it fell to you." Darcy placed his hand in the small of his wife's back as the three of them made their way down the hall.

"Your father left instructions for Mrs. Reynolds to prepare a suite for you and Mrs. Darcy. She has kept you in the same wing but further down the hall. You have essentially the same view. If either of you wish it, I can ask her to open one on the other side of the passage."

Darcy glanced at Elizabeth. "I prefer the view from the side we are on, but I will leave the decision up to my wife." They had reached the stairs, and begun their descent.

"What is the view?"

"The woody hills behind the house. There is a bit of the gardens in the foreground but most of what we can see is forest, unless we are standing at the actual window."

"And, the other side?" Elizabeth kept her hand on the rail as she tried to keep up with

Darcy and Smith, who seemed to be descending at a faster pace than she was.

"The other side is the formal gardens. Very regimented, and often full of gardeners and whoever else my father may have invited. It is not as private, or does not feel so to me." Darcy reached the bottom step and nodded to Smith, who hurried away in the direction of the bedrooms.

"Oh." Elizabeth reached the bottom and accepted Darcy's arm. "I think, in light of the situation, that I would prefer the more private rooms."

Darcy breathed a sigh of relief. "Excellent. As soon as I see Smith again, I will tell him so." He escorted Elizabeth down the hall toward the open door on the right-hand side. "Pemberley is laid out much like Darcy House, but with more rooms," he explained as they walked. "There are three single person rooms in between each suite, and there is a suite in each corner of the wing. There are three wings: the family's rooms are to the left at the top of the stairs, this wing houses a mix of family and guests, and the hall to the right leads to guest chambers. The family rooms are actually set up in a different formation than the rest of the chambers, and there are fewer of them."

Elizabeth nodded to indicate she was listening, but her attention was caught by the large window at the end of the hall. She let go of Darcy's arm and walked toward it. "Why is that?"

Darcy shrugged and followed his wife to the end of the hall. He stopped beside her, tucking his arm around her with his hand at her waist. "I do not know. I suspect the ancestor who built the house enjoyed entertaining." He turned to look down the hall, letting go of Elizabeth in the process. "This is not the original house. The first one burned to the ground in 1492. It was not as large, as I understand it."

Elizabeth followed Darcy's gaze as she listened, then turned back to the window. "It is much larger than Longbourn, that is certain." She chuckled. "My father told me once that our home used to be larger, but that a fire destroyed half the house one winter a hundred years or so ago and it was never rebuilt. There is an odd doorway that leads to nowhere in the upstairs hall." She turned around again. "Apparently, it was sealed shut, but unlike the rest of the house, was never bricked over." She shrugged, her eyes twinkling.

Darcy laughed. "Does Longbourn have secret passageways?"

Elizabeth stilled, her eyes going wide. "No. Does Pemberley?"

Laughing again, Darcy tilted his head toward the window. "Did you enjoy the view?"

"I did!" Elizabeth smiled and turned back. "Perhaps we can visit that folly at some point in our stay?"

"We can, if you wish it." Darcy held out his arm again. "Come; our bathwater is getting cold." He led his wife in through the open doorway into a sitting room, shutting and locking the wooden panel behind him. Looking right and then left, he gestured for her to remain where she was, then entered the door to the right. Within seconds, he returned and escorted her through the portal on the left side of the chamber. "This is my bed-chamber." He nodded toward the door on the other side of the room. "My dressing room is through that door."

Elizabeth looked around at the décor. "It is a nice room."

Darcy's eyes followed her gaze. "It is. Not terribly masculine, but it was probably not decorated with any one person or sex in mind."

"No, probably not. Perhaps we can ask to redecorate a bit? Some darker colors would do, I should think."

"I will make the request." Darcy lifted and lowered a shoulder. "That is all we can do."

"I understand." Elizabeth smiled, then turned back toward the sitting room. "Since you said these were your rooms, am I to assume mine are on the other side of the sitting room?"

"Yes. Let me show you." Darcy took his wife's hand and led her through to her bedchamber. "It is decorated similarly. I believe Mrs. Reynolds probably assigned you this room because it is closer to the stairs, and thus the nursery."

Elizabeth nodded. She was wandering the edges of the room, running her hand over the fine desk and chair in one corner, and admiring the bedside table. She turned to look at Darcy. "In light of your … assignment …" She stopped, not sure how to go on. "I –" She sighed. "I do not know how to ask this without seeming like a wanton, so I will just say it. I have gotten used to sleeping with you, and as I am not yet with child, as far as we know, I am wondering if you truly wish us to sleep apart?" Her skin was a fiery red by the time she was done speaking.

Darcy smiled and approached. He grasped her hands, which she was squeezing together in front of her. "I do wish to sleep with you. I have grown too used to having you in my bed to even contemplate spending the night alone. I propose that you use your dressing room for its purpose and we sleep in my chamber."

Elizabeth smiled, relaxing at his words. "I like the sound of that." She cocked her head as the sound of water splashing reached her ears. "Jenny is probably ready for me. Shall I meet you in the sitting room when I am finished?"

"Yes, and before I forget … keep the doors locked. I will explain later. Do not worry about the servants … they have their own entrances, and keys to our rooms." Darcy kissed Elizabeth before spinning around and heading to his own bath.

Chapter 10

Half an hour later, Darcy and Elizabeth met in their shared sitting room. Darcy had unlocked the door for a pair of servants carrying trays just before his wife entered, and the two were still setting out plates and silverware when he held the chair out for her. When the maids were finished, he took up his place across from her at the small table.

"It smells delicious." Elizabeth sniffed appreciatively as Darcy uncovered the plates and she poured tea for them both.

"Pemberley's cook is the best in the area. You will find anything else to be swill compared to meals here."

Elizabeth picked up her fork and lifted a bite of the mutton stew. She put it in her mouth and groaned. When she had chewed and swallowed, she agreed with Darcy's assessment. "You were right. I have never tasted the like." She dug in again, and the next several minutes were silent except for sounds of silverware clinking on plates and noises of appreciation for the exceptional meal.

When they were done eating and had pushed their plates away, Darcy began to load up the trays. He started to speak, explaining some of the things he had said earlier. "I never replied when you asked if Pemberley had secret passages." He glanced at Elizabeth, saw he had her attention, and continued. "In the family wing, where my father's rooms are, there are hidden doors to each of the dressing rooms. I suppose they are only secret to guests. To a young boy with an active imagination, they were fascinating." He shrugged as he resumed his seat and pulled his rapidly cooling tea towards him. "The doors lead to short staircases that in turn lead to passages on lower floors, which end at the kitchens. When these two wings were built, which I believe took some years after the family wing was completed, the decision was made to have one entrance per wing. The doors are hidden behind tapestries, one near the stairs and one further down the hall in the guest wing."

"How fascinating! Did you play in them as a boy?" Elizabeth arched a brow and smirked.

Darcy chuckled. "I did, as often as I could get away with it." The pair was silent for a moment until Darcy yawned. "I am sorry. The anxieties and inconveniences of the last few days seem to have caught up with me." He paused. "I was wondering if you noticed anything about Miss Robinson's behavior when we visited the schoolroom?"

Elizabeth set down her cup, which she had just emptied. "I did, as a matter of fact. If I did not know better, I would say she resents me for marrying you. Did she, perhaps, set her cap at you?"

Darcy rolled his eyes. "In a manner of speaking, I suppose she did. She would not have been opposed to compromising me, I am certain. I have long suspected that she was urged by my father to seduce me and report back anything I said or did. He would do that without a qualm."

"I am sorry. He is a hateful man." Elizabeth played with the corner of her napkin, folding and unfolding it. "I wanted to thank you for defending me to her. I know that could potentially put you in a difficult position."

"You are welcome. I could do no less. Of all the servants that I know or suspect are loyal only to my father, Miss Robinson is the only one who so thoroughly disgusts me. She was raised the daughter of a minor gentleman. She is educated. She cannot say she does not understand the ramifications of what she is doing."

"You said before there are fewer servants here who are blindly loyal to Mr. Darcy. Are there any I should specifically watch out for?"

Before Darcy could reply, Mr. Smith knocked on the door between the sitting room and Darcy's bedroom. When Darcy bid him enter, he obeyed, carrying a missive in his hand.

"Sir, this was handed to me by a footman. I was told to deliver it immediately." Smith extended the letter to his master.

Darcy accepted the note and dismissed his valet. He looked at the direction in disgust.

"Who is it from?" Elizabeth suspected she knew, from her husband's mien, but asked anyway.

"My father." Darcy drummed the edge of the table with the folded missive. "I wonder if I should wait until after we visit Georgiana to read it, or if I should open it now."

Elizabeth licked her lips. "That is a difficult decision. If the words within make you angry, will you be able to hold it in check when you see your sister?"

"I do not know. Possibly not."

"Then, why do we not visit her now and when we come back, you can read the letter? Unless he is here, your father surely will not know if you waited an hour to read it."

Darcy considered Elizabeth's words for a long moment. "That is true. Smith would have known if Father were in residence, or even if he had just arrived, and would have told me so. He has long been my intermediary of sorts; my protector, if you will. He said nothing, so I can safely assume Father is still in London, or perhaps on the road." He stood, tucking the note into his pocket. "It is yet early, but let us go see Georgiana. She will not mind if we have to leave before she gets in bed."

Elizabeth rose, accepted Darcy's hand, and walked with him to the schoolroom. It was empty, so he led her through the room to the right and down a short hall. There they found a set of smaller rooms, and Georgiana in one, dressed for bed and playing with a doll.

"Georgiana." Darcy's quiet voice drew his sister's attention away from her activity.

"Brother! Have you come to read me a story?" She jumped up and ran to Darcy, hugging him as she had earlier.

Darcy returned Georgiana's embrace. "I have. I brought Elizabeth with me."

"Will she read to me, as well?" The little girl looked up adoringly at her brother.

"You will have to ask her that question, but I cannot imagine she would say no. She did tell you she wished to be friends." Darcy pulled a little on his sister's braid.

Georgiana turned to Elizabeth. "Will you read to me, too? Fitzwilliam is an excellent reader, but I do not wish to wear him out."

Elizabeth laughed, Darcy along with her. "Of course, I will read to you. I love to read."

"Me, too!" Georgiana threw her arms around Elizabeth's waist. "Well, I cannot read very much yet, but I do love to listen when other people read to me."

"Come on then, Squirt. Climb into bed and we will each read you a story." Darcy looked around. "Where is Miss Robinson?"

Georgiana shrugged. "I do not know. Sometimes she gets me ready for bed and leaves me alone as you have found me, and I put myself to bed."

Darcy's brows rose. "I see." He looked at Elizabeth, meeting her eyes and seeing that she shared his feelings in the matter.

With Georgiana settled in bed with two books, Darcy and Elizabeth settled down on either side of her, leaning against the headboard. Georgiana handed each of them a book, then settled in to listen.

By the time the second book was finished, the girl was sound asleep. Darcy and Elizabeth rose, kissed her on the forehead, and tiptoed out of the room. They were silent as they walked down the hall and through the schoolroom. They had almost reached the door when it suddenly opened, and in crept the governess. She jumped and cried out when she turned from quietly closing the panel to see the couple standing there.

"Where have you been?" Darcy's harsh voice was pitched low. "You are charged with my sister's safety. You left her alone. Alone. Anything could have happened. She is eight years old."

"I -" The young woman stammered, clearly unnerved by Darcy's unexpected appearance.

"Never mind. Do not tell me." Darcy gestured for the governess to move away from the door. "Rest assured, my father will be informed of your misstep." Without allowing Miss Robinson to respond, he pulled Elizabeth through the door and into the hallway.

A few minutes later, they arrived back at their sitting room. Darcy let them in with a key he pulled from his waistcoat. He handed the key to his wife, and once they had entered, locked the door behind them. He strode to the window, leaning against the frame and running his hand through his hair.

Elizabeth decided to give her husband a few minutes to gather himself. She began to light the lamps placed around the room, as the sun had fallen low enough in the sky that it failed to give off enough light to see by. When she finished, she joined him at his post. "Will you inform your father about the governess?"

"I must, though I doubt it will do any good." He sighed. "I hate this. I hate living like this." He spun away from the window, cursing under his breath. He stood with his hands on his hips for a moment, then pulled the letter out of his pocket. "I suppose I should get this over with."

"Yes." Elizabeth moved to the settee in front of the cold fireplace. She patted the seat beside her. "Come and sit. There is a lamp here on the table that is bright enough that you should see what he says easily enough."

Darcy did as Elizabeth bid, settling into the corner of the furniture. With a sigh, he opened the missive and silently began to read. "He says your pin money is with the steward and that you are to visit the dressmaker in Lambton for a new wardrobe." He glanced up to see his wife nod. "He should set up an account for you. Instead, he makes you use your pin money." He shook his head in disgust.

"Do not fret about it. Truly." Elizabeth laid her hand on Darcy's arm when he opened his mouth to protest. "If we were in a different situation, you could speak to him, but we are not. One day, he will be gone and you will be master. If you wish to set accounts up for me at that time, you may. Until then, I will make do, as I always have. Growing up at Longbourn, I became very good at remaking gowns. Trust me."

Darcy gave his wife a skeptical look, but nodded. He turned his attention back to the letter. He read it all the way through, growing redder as he did. Without being aware of it, he clenched his jaw and began grinding his teeth. Suddenly, he leaped off the couch with a growl. "That -, that -, I hate him!" His shout drew Elizabeth to her feet. When she saw Smith in the bedroom doorway, she asked him with her eyes what to do and, seeing his nod toward Darcy and the way he melted back into the bedroom, took it to mean she should try to soothe him.

"What does he say? Please, stop. You will hurt yourself." Elizabeth pulled at Darcy's arm when he struck the wall with his fist.

Darcy whirled. "Do not tell me what to do! I am sick to death of being told what to do!"

"I am not. I tried to keep you from hurting yourself." Elizabeth felt her heart begin to race as the anger from the last three days began to rise within her.

"Well, stop. Just stop." Darcy flung an arm out. "What I do to myself is none of your concern. As a matter of fact, nothing I do is any of your concern. All you are to me is a burden. It was not enough that I had to protect my sister. Now I am saddled with a wife I must protect, as well. Just what I need. And not even a wife I chose, but one thrust upon me."

"I did not ask to marry you." Elizabeth's fists clenched at her sides as she resisted the urge to pound them into his nose. "I am as much a victim here as you."

Darcy was past listening to what his wife said. Instead, he was deep into his own thoughts, and they began to pour forth unchecked. "Perhaps my father will use you, as well. That is it! He set me up for this. He will use whatever he has available and soon, you will be going to him as the servants do. As Miss Robinson does." He lifted the letter and read a line. "'Perhaps I will give her to my godson, if you are unable to fulfill your assignment, as I suspect you are. George would be happy with such a comely wife, and he is much better suited to be master of Pemberley, anyway.'"

Elizabeth gasped but Darcy was too caught up to hear it. He turned on her. "I should send you to him now." He sneered. "That will show him I am my own man. I will not allow anyone to use me like that."

Suddenly, Smith appeared between Darcy and his wife. "Sir, you must calm down." He glanced over his shoulder to see Elizabeth standing rigid, fighting tears.

"Mr. Darcy!" Elizabeth was both horrified and angered beyond reason. "I told you before that I took my vows seriously. I did not wish to marry you any more than you wished to be tied to me. If you do not believe that, if you think for one moment that I would allow such a despicable person as your father to use me in any manner, you are not only wrong, you are not the person I thought you to be. I can assure you, sir, that if I had not been forced to wed you, you would be the last man in the world I could ever be prevailed upon to marry."

"Mrs. Darcy ..." Smith's quiet plea broke through the red haze surrounding Elizabeth's awareness. She curtseyed and without another word, turned on her heel and entered her bedroom, locking the door behind her.

Chapter 11

The valet next urged his master to calm. "Becoming angry will not help your situation. Come; I will pour you a glass of port. You can rail at me all night, if you wish."

All the fight had fled out of Darcy when his wife had walked away. He sagged, still clutching the letter, and allowed Smith to steer him into the bedroom. He sank into the wingback chair in front of the fireplace, rested his elbow on the arm, and leaned his head into his hand. He could feel tears rising and tried to swallow them down. When his valet took the letter and pressed a tumbler of red wine into his hand, he accepted it, drinking the liquid straight down without pausing. He handed the glass back to Smith, who quietly refilled it and handed it back.

"Would you like to talk about it?" Smith asked the question that had led to many deep discussions over the years of his service to the younger Darcy.

"You can read it if you wish." Darcy transferred the drink from his left hand to his right. "He taunted me with Wickham."

"I see." Smith smoothed out the crumpled paper and read the three short paragraphs. Then, he sighed. "You lashed out."

"I did." Darcy's head was back in his hand, this time the left one, as he began to become aware of what had transpired in the last few minutes.

"How many times has he done this now?"

Darcy shook his head. "I do not know. I have lost count."

"It has made you angry before." Smith settled into the chair that matched Darcy's, knowing he would likely be there for a couple hours, at the least.

"You know it has. This time, though … this time it was worse." Darcy knocked back half the port in the glass.

"How so?" Smith knew from experience how to approach his employer.

"You read it. He insinuated things about Elizabeth." Darcy suddenly groaned as the realization of what he said to his wife began to penetrate his brain. "I lost my temper with Elizabeth."

"Yes, sir. You did."

Darcy closed his eyes, the anger draining out of him. "I have never treated a woman that way before. I am no better than the man who sired me."

Smith shook his head. "You are not like your father. Every one of us who walks the earth has done things we are ashamed of. None of us is perfect."

"But, she is my wife. She is … Elizabeth. She is the best thing that ever happened to me, and I told her …" Darcy groaned and threw his head back against the chair. "I am so stupid." He rose and threw the tumbler into the fireplace with all his might.

Smith cringed at the sight of all the little pieces of glass he would have to clean up later. "You are not stupid. Your actions and words certainly were, but you are not." He stood and stepped behind Darcy, who leaned against the mantel. "You made a mistake. It can be corrected."

Darcy shook his head. "I do not know that it can. Words cannot be taken back." He sniffed as tears began to fill his eyes. "I had a good future ahead of me with her, aside from my inheritance requirements. I threw that away. All because of my father." His knees gave out as he began to sob.

Smith caught Darcy and helped him to the bed. He made the younger man as comfortable as he could and pulled a blanket up over him. Then, he pulled a chair up to the bed and sat. When Darcy had cried all the tears he was capable of, Smith spoke.

"Do you see what happened?"

Darcy sniffed, wiping his nose on the handkerchief his valet tucked into his hand. "My father wrote me a letter, I lost my temper, and I alienated the woman I have come to love." He looked up. "My father hoped this would happen, did he not? He probably even planned on it happening."

Smith nodded sadly. "That is highly probable, yes. You fell right into his trap. Undoubtedly, the conditions of your travel from Glenmoor were calculated to stir your feelings. The letter was the capstone of the plan."

Darcy closed his eyes, more tears leaking out to roll down his cheeks. "I hurt her."

"You did." Smith paused, cocking his head to examine Darcy. "She said some ugly things, as well."

"I deserved them for entertaining, even for a moment, that she would fall prey to my father's schemes. She is nothing like any other woman I have ever met." Darcy heard his wife's voice in his head as she declared him the last man she would ever have married had she not been forced. He swallowed. "I do not know how to fix this. I need to make amends, but I have no idea how to begin."

"An apology is always a good idea."

"Yes, of course." Darcy peered at the clock on the mantel. "It is late. She is probably in bed."

Smith said nothing. Darcy looked at him sharply. "What do you know?"

"I know that Jenny knocked on the door just before I sat down. It seems Mrs. Darcy cried herself to sleep."

Darcy closed his eyes for a long moment. He swallowed. "I will not wake her." He made a noise, half chuckle and half huff. "We said earlier we would not need two bedrooms. I guess we were wrong."

Again, Smith remained silent.

Darcy sighed. "Go on to bed. I will try to rest and see if I cannot figure out a way to make this up to Elizabeth. Leave the port and a tumbler here."

Smith glanced toward the fireplace and the pile of shattered glass within but bowed. He moved the carafe and a clean tumbler to the bedside stand. "Shall I get you a nightshirt?"

Darcy shook his head. "No. I have become used to sleeping nude. I will be fine. Good night."

Smith bowed, murmuring a quiet good night, and left his employer to his regrets.

~~~***~~~
~~~

The next morning, Elizabeth woke to both an aching head and an aching heart. She lay quietly, memories of the argument she had had with her husband filling her thoughts. She closed her eyes, fighting tears. She heard Jenny enter the room.

"Mrs. Darcy?"

For a moment, Elizabeth considered ignoring her, but saw little point in delaying the inevitable. Though she had yet to figure out how she planned to handle seeing her husband again, she knew she could not remain abed all day. "I am awake."

"Would you like a bath this morning? A long soak always makes things seem brighter. To me." Jenny's voice was tremulous, with an affected cheerfulness.

"That would be lovely." Elizabeth sat up. "Would it be possible for some tea and scones to be delivered to the dressing room?"

"Of course. I will see to it immediately." Jenny curtseyed, then strode to the bell and rang it before moving into the dressing room. "Which gown would you like for today?" She called over her shoulder.

"I would like a fresh nightgown, but I suppose something appropriate for walking will do." Elizabeth stood and looked out the window. "I think I will take a long ramble about the gardens today, assuming I can leave my room without my husband seeing me."

Jenny said nothing, instead simply nodding and moving into the closet to pull out her mistress' one walking gown.

Elizabeth sighed and followed her maid into the dressing room. There, she sat at the small table and unknotted the rag holding her braid together. She untwisted the hair, then picked up her brush and began to run it through her long tresses. That task complete, she lowered the brush to the table and dropped her hands into her lap. She sat there, staring at her reflection, until Jenny caught her attention.

"The kitchen seems to have anticipated our needs. The footmen are on their way up with the buckets of hot water. I saw two enter the hall from the servant's stair." A brisk knock on the door announced their arrival, and Jenny rushed to the door to allow them to enter. Soon, the tub was filled with warm, scented water, and Elizabeth was stepping in.

"Well, Lizzy," she said to herself once Jenny had left her to bathe. "This is a fine kettle of fish you have found yourself in." She sighed. "I will not cry," she whispered fiercely, as the hurt feelings and anger of last night threatened to overwhelm her again. "If that is truly how he feels, he does not deserve my tears." She sniffed. "I do not wish to see him. Let him stew in his own juices for a while." She laughed cynically. "Not that I think he's stewing. No doubt he has already written his father a letter, offering to send me to town." She shook her head. "I thought he was different."

A voice echoed in Elizabeth's mind, her grandmother's voice, giving a very young Elizabeth advice after she had fought with one of her sisters. "Think of the past only as it gives you pleasure. Yes, your sister did wrong by you, but she was caught up in the moment. She will soon come to regret what she did, and you must forgive and forget. Remember the good things about being her sister and forget the bad."

Elizabeth sighed. "I will try, but it is difficult. I do not feel like forgiving him right now. I am too hurt." She leaned back in the tub and closed her eyes. "And too angry, frankly." She sighed again as the thought occurred to her that she must forgive quickly and without considering her own feelings, lest an accident happen and she die with unforgiveness in her heart. "Very well," she said to the room. "I choose to forgive him, but I do not have to remain in the same room he is in.

I do not have to speak to him or anything else. I forgive him, but I plan to avoid him for a while."

It became clear to Darcy that his wife was ignoring him by the time dinner was served and he had not seen her. He sat at the table, an empty service beside him, in the place Elizabeth should have been. When Mrs. Reynolds peeked into the dining room to check on the footmen who were serving, he called her to his side.

"Yes, sir?"

"Mrs. Darcy was called down?" Darcy gestured to his wife's place setting.

Mrs. Reynolds flushed and twisted her hands together. "Yes, sir, she was. She requested a tray in her rooms."

Darcy nodded slowly. "I see." He sighed. "That is all." He watched the housekeeper curtsey and almost run from the room. He applied himself to his meal at that point, and after, climbed the stairs to his own chambers.

For the next two days, Elizabeth successfully avoided Darcy. She kept mostly to her rooms, except for a daily stroll around the gardens. She eyed the folly with longing, but felt pain at the reminder that her husband was supposed to show it to her himself. He might never do it now.

The one thing Elizabeth had a large amount of during her self-imposed exile was time to think, and think she did. She replayed the argument over and over in her mind. She started to feel ashamed for losing her temper and speaking in an unguarded fashion. *Much like my mother, that,* she thought with chagrin. Worse, she felt fear beginning to creep into her consciousness.

What Elizabeth feared was her future. Would she be forever estranged from her husband, whom she now realized she had been falling in love with? What would happen to her? Would he leave her here at Pemberley, and at his father's mercy? Was he serious when he said he would send her to be that other fellow's wife? She knew nothing of law, though she was aware that divorce was so difficult as to be impossible for all but the wealthiest few. She was also aware that annulment was out of the question. Both had given their correct names, as far as she knew, and neither was insane or unable to perform their duty.

The best she could hope for, Elizabeth decided, was to be sent back to Longbourn. That was fraught with its own problems, of course. Her family might not wish her back, and if they did, her mother's nerves would never allow her to forget that she had failed the family.

With these thoughts weighing on her mind, Elizabeth became restless. She hated that the situation was unresolved, but was both stubborn enough and prideful enough to demand that Darcy make the first move toward reconciliation. She did not think she could face rejection calmly and resolved to not put herself forward to be the first to apologize. While this headstrong disdain made her feel superior, it also led to depressed spirits and a lack of sleep.

Therefore, on the morning of the fourth day following the argument, when her breakfast tray contained a letter and a small package wrapped in bright paper and a ribbon, Elizabeth cried. Wiping her tears, she first lifted the note, running her finger over her name, written in a bold hand that had to be Darcy's. She snapped the seal and unfolded it, her hands shaking. Swallowing, she wiped her eyes again and began to read.

Dearest Elizabeth,

Be not alarmed that I will repeat the words I spoke to you a few nights ago. I am ashamed at the memory of them, and more so at the knowledge that I would give you so much pain. I am sorry, heartily sorry, and I ask you to search your heart and, if you can find it within you to do so, to forgive me.

It did not take long after you fled to your rooms for me to realize that I had treated you abominably. I said things to you that would make my father proud and in a manner that was more reminiscent of him than of the gentleman I have striven for years to become. I worked hard for a long time to emulate good men, but in a moment of temper threw it all away. Elizabeth, your husband is a stupid man.

You said to me that you would never have married me were you not forced to, even if I had been the last man on earth. I do not blame you for feeling this way. However, if you choose to forgive me and allow me a second chance, I vow to never repeat such ugly behavior again.

Along with this note, I have sent you a small token of my esteem. It is not part of Pemberley's collection; it was purchased with you in mind, not as a way to buy your affection, which I doubt I ever could, anyway, but as a method of demonstrating to you how much you mean to me.

Though I wish I could say this to you the first time face to face, I cannot, nor am I entirely certain how you will respond, but I cannot hold back. I have come to love you, with all my heart. I hope you can forgive me, but if you cannot, I will simply love you from afar. Rest assured, I will continue to protect and care for you, regardless of your decision.

Your loving and repentant husband,

FD

Chapter 12

Elizabeth's hand came up over her mouth as she read, and as she finished, she sobbed. She read the missive again, then held it to her chest and lifted her face, a silent prayer of thanks rising to heaven. Then, her hand still shaking, she laid the note to the side of her tray and picked up the box.

She pulled at one end of the ribbon, untying the knot, and laying the length of purple satin aside. Next, she pulled the paper away and lifted the top of the small, square box. Inside, nestled on a bed of velvet, was a ring with a large amethyst stone surrounded by small diamonds. The white of the smaller stones set off the purple in the larger one in an aesthetically pleasing manner.

"Oh, my." Elizabeth breathed the words as she picked up the exquisitely crafted ring. She slipped it over the ring finger of her right hand, but it was just loose enough that she feared losing it. It was too small for her middle finger. Disappointed, she thought for a long moment before slipping off her wedding ring, sliding the new one on her finger, and replacing the gold band. "There," she murmured, satisfied that the wedding band would hold the new ring in place.

Elizabeth lifted the letter again and read it a third time. She became swamped with the feeling of shame that had plagued her the last day or two. She cried again. "Of course, I will forgive him! How could I not? My behavior was no better than his." She closed her eyes. "How can he tell me he loves me, after what I said?" Before despair could get a firm grasp on her feelings, she read the part of the letter where her husband declared himself. She took a deep breath, comforted by his words, and stood. She strode to the other side of the table and seated herself there. She pulled the writing desk towards her and opened it, taking out a sheet of paper, the ink bottle, and a quill. She trimmed the pen and opened the ink as she mentally composed her message. Then, carefully, so as not to waste paper, wrote out a reply. When she was finished, she read it over. She sighed when she spotted a place that needed to be reworded. She crossed it out and wrote in new words, then read it over once more. Finally satisfied, she took out a clean sheet of paper and slowly and ever-so-carefully rewrote the words. When she was done, she sanded it, folded the page, and warmed the sealing wax, dripping some over the edge and allowing it to cool. She wrote Darcy's name on the outside, then picked the letter up and took it back to her tray. She picked up her cup, wrinkling her nose at the cold tea.

Elizabeth hummed to herself as she broke her fast. When her abigail returned to take the tray, she handed the girl the letter. "Will you see that this is handed to Mr. Darcy, right away? You may give it to Mr. Smith if you must. I know he will see to it that my husband receives it, but you are to give it to no one else."

Jenny accepted the missive. "I will, ma'am. Is there anything else I can do for you?"

The corners of Elizabeth's lips lifted, the first genuine smile she had worn in the three days since the argument with Darcy. "When you return from delivering that letter, I would like to change my gown. I would like to don the lilac day dress."

A slow smile spread over Jenny's face. "Very good, ma'am. I will just pop over to Mr. Darcy's rooms and be right back." She curtseyed and disappeared.

Elizabeth finished her breakfast as quickly as she could while Jenny completed her mission and laid out the dress. After washing her face and hands, she allowed the maid to undo her buttons and slip her out of the walking gown and into the purple one. She examined her reflection, feeling hope for the first time in days.

~~~***~~~

Darcy had spent the period of his wife's seclusion in an agony of feeling. He often berated himself for his behavior and vowed that he would do better. He was torn between tracking her down and giving her space. Smith assured him she would speak to him again when she was ready, but Smith had never been married. What did he know of women and their ways? When he expressed this to his valet, the servant rolled his eyes. Darcy knew he should probably rebuke the other man for it, but could not. If Smith was making faces, then Darcy knew he had some more thinking to do.

The young man resolved to stay away from Elizabeth as long as he could or until she gave him some indication that she welcomed his presence. This resolve lasted until he came upon Jenny and Smith discussing her.

"How is my wife?" Darcy demanded the information, rather than requesting it.

Jenny glanced at Smith as she curtseyed. "She is …" The maid hesitated.

Smith spoke before Jenny could finish. "She is not sleeping, sir. Jenny tells me she is listless and unsettled."
~~~

Darcy's eyes snapped from his valet to his wife's maid. "Is this true? Is she suffering?"

"I should probably not break her confidence, sir, but yes, it is true." Jenny bit her lip. She thought a moment and then said, "I think her heart is broken; she is definitely worried and frightened."

Darcy's eyes widened. "She is frightened? That is it." He turned to Smith. "I cannot stay away and allow her to fret. I must apologize." He spun on his heel and paced away, missing the pleased look Smith and Jenny shared. "If she refuses to see me, I cannot do it in person. I must write her a letter." He turned around again, intending to head to his writing desk, already composing his note in his mind.

"If you please, sir." Jenny's soft words captured Darcy's attention. "When my parents argued, my Papa often brought my Mama a present. He was a blacksmith, and one time, he made her a tiny ring with a heart on it. Mama instantly forgave him. She said any man who took the time to create something that delicate was surely sorry for what he had done."

Darcy's brow creased. "He gave her a present?" When Jenny nodded, he bit his lip. "I am not a blacksmith. I have no skills, even in working with wood."

"It does not have to be something you created, sir." Smith watched Darcy carefully to see if he understood. "As long as the gift is chosen with the receiver in mind, a purchased one is just as valuable."

"Do you think so?" Darcy's eyes darted from the valet to the wall and back. "I could buy her something?"

"Yes, sir, you could."

Darcy began to pace again. "What could I get her? She likes to read; I could buy her a book. I know nothing of ribbons, but she says she does not care about fashion. Wait!" He spun around to look at the servants. "You said your father created a ring for your mother. I could buy my wife one. Not with a heart on it, though. Not that a heart would not be meaningful." He looked apologetically at Jenny, who shrugged and smiled.

Darcy looked at Smith. "Have my horse saddled. I am going into Lambton. I believe the jeweler is still in with the watch maker?"

"He is, sir." Smith strode to the pull and rang the bell. When a footman appeared in the doorway, he gave the other man instructions. Then, he handed Darcy his hat, gloves, and riding crop, which he had retrieved from the wardrobe. "Here you are. Good luck."

Darcy nodded to Smith and Jenny and without a word, hurried out of his rooms and down the hall.

The next morning, he awoke with the sun, eager to deliver to Elizabeth the ring he had purchased and the note he had spent half the night composing. He dressed quickly, seeking Jenny out and handing her the items with instructions to add them to his wife's breakfast tray. Then, he went out for a long, hard ride to dispel some of his nervousness.

When Darcy came back in to bathe, a letter was waiting, addressed to him in a feminine hand. His heart skipped several beats. It was all he could do not to rip it open right then and there, but he reasoned with himself that if her reply was favorable, she might not wish to be hugged by a man smelling of sweat and horse.

Darcy rushed through his bath, dressing with dizzying speed and hurrying Smith along through his shave. When the valet was finally finished, Darcy stood from the shaving chair and walked across to the dresser, where the letter from Elizabeth lay, teasing him. He picked it up, his heart again speeding. He swallowed to moisten his suddenly dry mouth, then moved into the bedroom and took a seat in front of the window. He looked up, sending a silent prayer to heaven for a favorable response and then, before his courage could desert him, he broke open the seal and unfolded the missive.

Dear Husband,

It was with both pleasure and shame that I received your letter and gift. Before I say aught else, I must apologize for my intemperate speech and conduct during our disagreement three nights ago. I have no excuse. Regardless of how my feelings may have been wounded, I had no right to behave so rudely and insensitively to you. I am sorry, and I beg your forgiveness.

I accept your apology with a glad heart. Thank you for making it. I chose to forgive you the night of our argument, but your words have gone a long way toward healing my heart and that superficial forgiveness is now firmly embedded, your mistakes completely forgiven.

Thank you, too, for your assurances in regards to my future. Knowing I can rely on you in the years to come eases my mind.

Let me now thank you for the beautiful ring. I adore it and am even now admiring how it shines on my finger. Thank you, Husband.

I have come to realize over the last few days that I love you. I had feared all hope of receiving your affection was lost. Thank you for that gift, as well. My heart sings to know that you love me, too.

Will you walk with me through the gardens this morning, if you are not needed elsewhere?

Love,

ED

A slow smile lifted Darcy's lips as he read his wife's words of forgiveness and affection. He leaped up from his chair with a whoop and raced to the dressing room door. "Smith!"

The valet looked up from his task. "Yes, sir?" He stood.

"Send word to the steward. He is to send Mrs. Darcy's pin money up to me here, and he will have to address the drainage issue at the Miller farm on his own. I am spending today with my wife. As a matter of fact, inform Mr. Wickham that he will be on his own the rest of the week."

"As you wish." Smith bowed and, once Darcy had disappeared out the door again, sat back down with a growing smile on his face.

Darcy ran back into his bedchamber, stopping at his portable writing desk and unlocking it.

He unlocked a small drawer within the wooden box. Then, he kissed Elizabeth's note and carefully placed it inside. He closed and locked the drawer, then shut and locked the lid. He raced to the door that led to the sitting room and paused with his hand on the latch. He took a silent assessment of himself, pulling his waistcoat down and smoothing a hand over his freshly pomaded hair. He opened the door and, seeing no Elizabeth, strode across to her bedroom. There, he paused again, taking a deep breath and willing his nerves to subside. Finally, he lifted his hand and knocked. When he heard his wife's voice bid him to enter, he slowly depressed the latch and stuck his head in the room.

"May I come in?"

Elizabeth stood at the end of the bed, hands clasped in front of her, in a lilac colored gown he had admired on her before. A tremulous but welcoming smile graced her lips. "Please, do."

Darcy slid into the room, gently closing the door behind him. He stepped across the space, stopping in front of his wife, and held out his hand. When she placed hers on top of it, relief flowed through him. "I am so sorry." His eyes searched hers. "Can you ever forgive me?"

Elizabeth's eyes filled with tears. "I will, if you can forgive me. I already have."

"There is nothing to forgive, my love." Darcy's hands rose to rest on her shoulders, his thumbs caressing her jaw. "I swear to you, I will never behave like that in front of you again. I will never purposely be hurtful to you. I love you." His words ended on a whisper as he bent his head to capture her lips. When he felt Elizabeth's arms slide around his waist, he dropped his hands to wrap around her and pull her close. When he reached the point that he needed to breathe or pass out, he pulled back, resting his forehead against hers.

"I love you." Elizabeth whispered the words. She clung to him.

Darcy captured his wife's lips once more. Before long, their passion overtook them and he picked her up, one arm behind her shoulders, the other under her knees, and carried her around to the side of the bed.

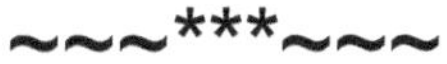

Hours later, Darcy awakened, Elizabeth in his arms, her head resting on his shoulder. He could see his dressing gown draped over the foot of the bed and the clothing he had donned after his ride carefully draped over a chair. Looking toward the other side of the bed, his wife's things were similarly cared for. He knew he had been exhausted and that Elizabeth likely had been, too. He recalled the dark circles under her eyes as she had stood there in her purple dress. A stab of guilt and regret hit him, and he kissed her head. He was soon sleeping again.

The couple spent the rest of the day in bed or in their sitting room in their dressing gowns. They slept, talked, ate, and made love, then did it all over again.

"Should we go up to see your sister?" Elizabeth asked the question as they ate the meal the cook had sent up for them.

Darcy shook his head. "I warned her last evening that she might not see me today. I promised her a picnic tomorrow. I thought you might not mind."

"Not at all! I love picnics." Elizabeth's enthusiasm brought a smile to her husband's face. "I think I should invite her to tea one afternoon, as well."

"She would like that. She needs to be influenced by more than just that governess." Darcy took a sip of tea. "I sent a message to my father, informing him of what we discovered a few nights ago. He should have received it by now. If he decides to write back, we will know in another day or two, I should imagine."

"What do you think his reaction will be?" Elizabeth speared a piece of fish and popped it into her mouth.

"I hope he finds a new governess. What I believe he do is will tell me to mind my own affairs." Darcy shrugged. "He seems to care less for my sister than he does even for me. I should be grateful he leaves her out of his schemes and forget the rest. I am pulled in two directions, wishing to both protect her and improve her situation. It often seems hopeless."

"You are doing the best you can. That is all that matters." Elizabeth pushed her plate away and picked up her tea, placing her elbows on the table. She looked at Darcy over the top of the cup.

"I am; at least, I hope I am." He shrugged again. When Elizabeth placed her cup back into its saucer, he extended his arm across the table, palm up. She immediately placed her hand in his and he tightened his fingers around hers, drawing her up and around the small table. At the same time, he pushed his chair back. He pulled Elizabeth down onto his lap, grinning when she giggled.

Chapter 13

The next day, Darcy and Elizabeth entered the schoolroom to find an excited Georgiana ready and waiting for them. Darcy dismissed Miss Robinson, telling her to feel free to spend the afternoon as she wished, as long as she returned in time for her charge's dinner. Then, with his sister between himself and Elizabeth and holding their hands, he led his family down the stairs and out of the house.

The trio followed the front drive around the house to the gardens, followed by a group of footmen carrying baskets and blankets.

"Where are we going?" Georgiana skipped between her brother and new sister.

"I thought we might visit the folly. There is a nice, flat area behind it that receives sun most of the day." Darcy glanced over his sister's head to Elizabeth in time to catch her look at him with delight written over her features. "What say you, Mrs. Darcy?"

"I say it sounds wonderful." Elizabeth's smile lit up her countenance.

"Excellent." Darcy turned his gaze forward, guiding his wife and sister around the corner, through the gardens, and up the path to the small stone structure.

When they had arrived and chosen the perfect spot to have their picnic, Darcy instructed the servants to set things up while he and the ladies explored the folly. Elizabeth and Georgiana were disappointed that it was empty inside, but spent the next quarter hour weaving a fine tale to explain the structure, its appearance at Pemberley, and the reasons for its current state of desolation.

When everything was ready for them, the three sat on a blanket and partook of the bread, cheese, and other delicious foods Cook had prepared. They followed that with cups of cider. Then, Elizabeth read books to her sister. Darcy, sated and drowsy, allowed himself to fall asleep.

"Mrs. Darcy?" Georgiana's quiet question interrupted Elizabeth's story.

The older girl smiled. "Why do you not call me Elizabeth, as your brother does? Or even Lizzy, as my sisters do? Mrs. Darcy is so formal, and as I said before, I would dearly love for us to be friends."

Georgiana thought about that for a moment. "I think I would like that," she finally declared. "I have never had a sister before. Will you teach me how?"

"I will." Elizabeth winked. "The first thing you must do is decide which of my names you will call me."

Georgiana put her finger to her mouth, biting on the tip, as she thought again. "I will call you …" She dragged the words out with a giggle. "I will call you Elizabeth, because that is what Brother calls you. But, I might sometimes call you Sister. Will you mind that much?"

"Not at all! I would be honored by the name." Elizabeth reached over to smooth back a lock of hair that had fallen across her new sister's cheek.

"May I ask you a question?" Georgiana looked down and picked at a piece of lint on the blanket.

"You may." Elizabeth tilted her head. "Is something the matter?"

Georgiana shrugged, looking over at her still-sleeping brother. "Fitzwilliam told me that you did not come see me earlier because he was churlish with you." She looked up at Elizabeth, her brow creased. "He said you were angry with him."

Elizabeth sighed to herself. Darcy had told her what he said to his sister in answer to her questions. She was not certain the young girl needed to know everything, and she certainly did not wish to overstep her place or to begin a discussion that might be too much for Georgiana to bear. "He was. We argued, but you should know that we *both* said ugly things to each other. Ugly and unkind. We have apologized to each other and made amends." Elizabeth tilted her head as she examined her sister's expression. "Are you worried?"

"I was. He was so sad." Georgiana sighed. "I did not like seeing him that way." She leaned closer to Elizabeth, resting her hand on the older girl's leg. "He told me you were distressed, as well. He said that yesterday when he asked me if I would like to picnic with him. He said he bought you a gift as an apology and as a way to make up for his words."

Elizabeth smiled. "He did. Would you like to see it?"

Georgiana nodded eagerly. "Yes, please!"

Elizabeth held her hand out and allowed her sister to examine the ring.

"It is beautiful!" Georgiana whispered the words, reverence in her tone.

"It is. It is also my favorite color, and your brother knew that. I want you to understand, however, that it was not the ring that made me forgive him." Elizabeth waited for Georgiana to look up. When she was certain she had the girl's attention, she continued. "Fitzwilliam also wrote me a letter, in which he apologized for his words and behavior. What he said in that note was sincere; I understood from what he wrote to me that he was sorry he had done what he did."

Georgiana nodded. "So, when I do something wrong, I need to apologize instead of trying to do things for the person I wronged."

"That is it, exactly. Without your brother's note, I may have not realized that he meant what he said, and I might have thought he was trying to sway me with expensive baubles. I would not have been able to overcome my feelings without it."

"Are you happy to be part of our family?" Georgiana's gaze searched Elizabeth's mien for clues.

"I am very happy to be married to your brother, and to be your sister." She tapped Georgiana's nose with her finger, smiling when the girl giggled.

Georgiana suddenly hopped up and threw her arms around Elizabeth, squeezing her tightly. "I am so happy you are my sister."

Elizabeth held Georgiana for a long time, whispering her agreement. Then, they separated and played quiet word games while Darcy napped.

That evening, as they walked down the steps to dinner, Darcy asked if his wife had enjoyed their outing.

"I did. Georgiana is such a sweet girl. She was worried about me and asked if I was happy to be a Darcy." Elizabeth kept her eyes on the steps she was descending but felt her husband's arm stiffen under her fingers. "I told her I was very happy to be her sister and your wife." As she and Darcy stepped off the final stair and onto the marble floor at the bottom, she felt him relax. He lifted her hand off his arm and kissed it. When he placed it back down, he twined his fingers with hers.

"I am glad," Darcy whispered, stopping to bend and kiss Elizabeth's lips.

<p style="text-align:center">~~~***~~~</p>

The next day, Darcy gave Elizabeth another riding lesson. He had been shocked in Scotland to learn that she knew only the basics of how to mount, dismount, urge the animal into a walk, and stop him. This time, after giving her a refresher on what she already knew and making her ride around the yard a few times, he had her dismount, handing the reins of the gentle mare to a stable boy to groom and put away. He had the largest saddle-trained horse Pemberley had, a gelded Shire horse named Cicero, readied and brought out. Then, he helped Elizabeth mount and climbed up behind her.

"Is this really a good idea?" Elizabeth glanced at the ground, swallowing at how far away it appeared to be. She clutched the edge of the saddle with one hand and her skirts with the other. She was mounted as though she were sidesaddle in front of her husband.

Darcy settled in behind her and pulled his wife closer into the cradle of his legs. "Yes, it is, if you wish to see as much of Pemberley as possible while we are still alone. Once we have attended church this Sunday, the neighbors will undoubtedly begin calling and we will have no peace the rest of our stay." As he spoke, he arranged Elizabeth to his satisfaction, urging her to face forward and lean back into him if she needed or wanted to. Then, one arm around her waist and his free hand holding the reins, he nudged Cicero into motion.

"We are not too heavy for him?" Elizabeth leaned back, feeling safer held as she was, close to her husband.

Darcy snorted. "Have you seen the size of this beast?" He shook his head. "Cicero could hold us both if you weighed twice what you do now." He squeezed her waist. "Trust me."

With a sigh, Elizabeth agreed to do just that. She forced her muscles to relax, leaning back against him.

The couple rode up the woody hills behind the house to the highest point on Pemberley. From there, they could see dozens of fields in a patchwork of sizes, shapes, and colors.

"That is Pemberley," Darcy said with pride. "As far as the eye can see."

"Oh, my!" Elizabeth put her hand to her chest. "It is huge!"

"It is one of the biggest estates in Derbyshire." Darcy grew quiet. A long moment later, he murmured, "As long as my father does not lose any of it."

"I hope he does not." Elizabeth squeezed the hand that was pressed into her belly, holding her steady.

After another long moment of silence, Darcy turned Cicero's head away from the edge of the outlook and into a large clearing that sat behind them. He stopped the gelding and dismounted, reaching up to help Elizabeth down. Leaving the horse with his reins trailing the ground, he led his wife to his favorite area to sit and watch the world, knowing Cicero would not leave the clearing.

The young couple sat for a long time, eating the lunch the cook had packed for them and talking. They discussed the future, both immediate and long-term, and their pasts. Finally, the sun moved far enough around the sky that they knew they must go home.

~~~***~~~

On Sunday, Darcy proudly escorted his wife and sister to the church in Kympton where his family had worshipped for centuries. He introduced her to the rector, Mr. Williams, and to as many of the members of the congregation as impeded their progress to the carriage when the service was over.

After church, the three spent the day together. The adults used the opportunity to review some of Georgiana's learning and etiquette, and to teach her a couple new things.

On Monday, Darcy's prediction about visitors came true. Nearly all the principal families in the area sent someone to meet the new Mrs. Fitzwilliam Darcy. Elizabeth handled every question with grace. None of the ladies, nor their daughters and husbands, were as calculating as Mrs. Little had been in Scotland, but the young bride treated each with caution. She did not know
~~~

any of these people well enough to know whom to trust and who not to.

By previous agreement between them, Elizabeth deferred to Darcy in regards to invitations to dine or attend other soirees. They did not know when his father might call them to town, though Darcy suspected it would be soon. Whenever an invitation was issued, Darcy put the issuer off with that excuse, but promised to host a dinner of his own when they returned, if his father allowed.

As it turned out, on Wednesday of that very week, the elder Darcy sent a tersely-worded missive to his son, commanding the couple to attend him in London.

Elizabeth sat with her husband in their sitting room, reading letters. She had written to her sister Jane the day of her arrival at Pemberley and had just received a reply. Darcy sat beside her, his own letters in his hand.

Darcy folded the note his cousin had sent him and picked up the next. "This one is from Father." He broke the seal with a sigh and began to silently read.

Elizabeth lowered her letter to her lap and watched the expressions crossing Darcy's face as he read. When he looked up, she inquired about the contents. "What does he say?"

Darcy shrugged. "He starts by rebuking me for telling him about the governess. I am to mind my own affairs – those are not his words but the sentiment is the same – and he will mind his. Which, of course, involve me." Darcy rolled his eyes.

"I am sorry." Elizabeth rubbed his arm. "Does he have any other wisdom to impart?"

"Yes." Darcy consulted the missive again. "We are to depart for London at dawn on Monday and are expected in town in time for tea on Friday. He has made arrangements at the usual inns along the way."

"Hm. Well, let us hope he made better ones than he did the last trip we took." Elizabeth rolled her own eyes and picked up her letter again.

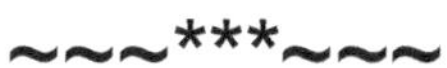

The rest of that week was spent returning visits, making sure to inform the neighbors of their departure, exploring Pemberley inside and out, and spending time with Georgiana. The young girl wished to accompany her sister and brother to town, but Darcy refused to allow it. He reminded her that if their father wished her to come, he would send for her, and that it was probably best that he did not. Georgiana accepted his words, though they caused her no little unhappiness.

The three attended church again on Sunday, and that night, when she was put to bed, Georgiana clung to Darcy and Elizabeth, crying. The couple felt bad to be leaving, but also felt they had no choice. When they were alone, they shed almost as many tears as their young sister had.

Chapter 14

The accommodations on the trip south were far better than the ones that had been provided between Scotland and Pemberley. That did not mean the trip was any easier.

The expected one night at an inn on Tuesday turned into two nights when the skies opened up and turned the roads into a sloppy, muddy mess. The rain had stopped by morning, but it took an entire day for the turnpike to become passable. Darcy and Elizabeth spent the entirety of Wednesday in their rooms, except for meals.

On Thursday, the group set out once more. The roads were boggy in parts, requiring the coach's passengers to get out and walk for brief times. It was during one of these periods near the end of the day's travels that a downpour suddenly overtook them. Darcy, Elizabeth, and their servants were soon soaked to the skin, their sodden clothing clinging to them. They reentered the coach as soon as possible, dripping water all over the fine upholstery.

It was clear, by the time the group reached the inn, that Elizabeth had caught a chill. She burrowed into Darcy's side under the blankets he had draped over them, but her shivering, once begun, did not cease.

Upon entering the inn, Darcy immediately ordered a hot bath for his wife, escorting her up the stairs to their rooms without waiting for acknowledgement. Once there, he began stripping her clothes off, ordering Jenny to prepare first for the bath and then a warm nightgown. When the tub arrived, he ordered it placed in front of the fire he had built up. Then, he arranged the room's screen so it held the heat in closer to the tub. He sent Smith to borrow an additional screen from an empty room and arranged it to further enclose the area around the fireplace. Through it all, Elizabeth shivered under a blanket in a chair placed as close to the roaring blaze as it could safely get.

Once he had everything arranged to his liking, Darcy helped Elizabeth into the tub. He sent Jenny off to change her clothes. "I will assist my wife. You go change and warm up. Order a bath for your room, as well, if you need to."

With a curtsey, Jenny left the room. Smith followed, after laying Darcy's dressing gown over one of the screens.

Darcy stripped, eager to remove his wet clothing. He then applied himself to assisting Elizabeth with her bath, including washing her hair. When she was clean and as warm as the water could make her, he helped her stand, wrapping her in clean towels and her dressing gown and seating her in the chair. He quickly bathed himself, rinsed with the clean water left warming on the hearth, and dried off. When he had donned his dressing gown, he dried her hair and brushed it out.

Despite her husband's ministrations and a night spent held closely in his arms under a pile of blankets, Elizabeth was unable to warm thoroughly. She slept restlessly.

The entirety of the following day, Elizabeth dozed off and on in Darcy's arms as they travelled the last leg of their journey. She was wrapped in blankets but still shivered now and then. She spoke little when she was awake. She was listless and tired. Her throat was scratchy, making swallowing painful.

"You will be well." Darcy rubbed his hand up and down Elizabeth's arm as he repeated the same words he had said one hundred times over the course of the day.

"It is only a trifling cold." Elizabeth croaked the words into her husband's waistcoat. "I will be right as rain in a day or two."

Darcy nodded, pressing his lips to her forehead. She was slightly warm, but not alarmingly so.

When the group arrived in London, Darcy helped Elizabeth descend from the carriage and up the steps into the house. Mrs. Bishop waited in the entry hall, and he instantly began to give her orders.

"Mrs. Darcy is unwell. I want the biggest bathtub in this house placed in her dressing room and filled with hot water for a bath. Immediately. Send up some chicken broth and tea, and a light meal."

Mrs. Bishop interrupted him. "Mr. George Darcy has ordered you to be moved to the third floor. You will be in the same corner of the house."

Darcy has stopped when the housekeeper began to speak. His only reaction was a press of his lips into a thin line. "Very well," he said. "My orders stand." Without waiting for the housekeeper to indicate her acceptance of his instructions, Darcy guided Elizabeth past her and up the stairs.

"Will that cause a problem?" Elizabeth stopped to catch her breath for a moment.

Darcy shrugged. "It could. My father generally insists on that tub remaining in his rooms. If he decides to bathe before you are finished, he could make a fuss about it." He began to move up the stairs again when Elizabeth stepped up.

"He demands an heir from our marriage; if he objects to my care in this instance, I will remind him of it." He was quiet for a few more steps. As they reached the top, he spoke again. "I have no doubt that he secretly hopes I will fail so he can hand my inheritance over to his favorite." He led his wife to the door of the rooms they had been assigned before.

"We will not fail, William." Elizabeth's raspy words made him pause in the act of opening the door. He looked down at her. "I promise you, we will not fail."

With a small smile, Darcy leaned down to kiss Elizabeth's forehead. "You cannot make a promise like that, but thank you." He led her into the room, shutting it behind him.

Though Darcy expected that he and Elizabeth would have to dine with his father downstairs, he never received a summons. He inquired of his valet about the matter.

"Your father sent word to the housekeeper that he was dining out this evening. She does not expect him home at all."

"Interesting." Darcy paused. "Very well, then. My wife and I will remain within our rooms tonight. Bring me up a bottle of my father's whiskey and some honey. She needs something to warm her up, and Mrs. Reynolds swears by it."

Smith inclined his head. "Very good, sir. Might I also suggest a bit of willow bark in some tea?"

"Yes; that is an excellent idea. Bring them up after we eat. I will try to get her in bed at an early hour. The combination of whiskey and willow bark ought to make her sleepy enough to be willing." Darcy glanced over his shoulder at the sound of Elizabeth's sneeze. "Some extra handkerchiefs would not go amiss, either." He looked at his valet once more. "Thank you."

Smith tipped his head again before turning smartly and exiting the room.

Eventually, Darcy got Elizabeth to drink some broth and then climb into bed. His prediction was correct. A shot of whiskey and honey, followed by a cup of willow bark tea, and she was ready for sleep. Darcy climbed in beside her, pulled her into his arms, and within minutes, she was snoring softly. He kissed her forehead and settled in, soon joining her in resting.

Darcy woke before his wife did the next day. Light was streaming through a crack between the curtain panels. He blinked and yawned, then pressed his lips to Elizabeth's head. Her skin was not any warmer than it should have been, for which he was grateful. When he felt her stir, he pulled away a bit so as to see her face. When her eyes blinked open, he smiled. "Good morning."

At her husband's quiet greeting, Elizabeth yawned, snuggling deeper into his embrace. "Good morning."

"How do you feel?"

Elizabeth mentally assessed herself. "My throat still hurts a little, but I think I feel better. My head does not seem to be full of wool this morning."

"Good." Darcy squeezed her briefly. "You slept better."

"I did." She peeked up at him. "I suspect that concoction you made me drink had something to do with it."

Darcy chuckled. "The whiskey and honey? Probably. You are clearly unused to strong drink."

"Imagine if I had consumed the entire glass." She shook her head, the hair that had fallen into her face clinging to the front of his nightshirt. She smirked to herself.

Darcy whispered his next words into Elizabeth's ear. "Perhaps another time." He kissed the curve and grinned when she shivered and sighed. "Do you feel well enough to get out of bed and dress?"

"I think so. I think I should try, anyway. I would not wish to be the cause of friction in the household."

Darcy was quiet for a long moment. "I am sorry. That should not even have to be a consideration for you."

Elizabeth lifted her face out of its warm nesting place so she could look at her husband and see his expression. "It is well. The situation will not last forever. At some point, you will come of age and we will be able to move to another."

"Yes, this is true." Darcy feared it was not and that as long as his father lived, he would be under the older man's thumb, but he did not speak those thoughts aloud. Before he could say anything else, a servant knocked on the dressing room door and he bid the person to enter. "Come."

Smith stepped into the room, approaching the bed with his eyes on his shoes. "Good morning, sir."

"Good morning. What news do you have?" Darcy pulled the comforter up higher, until only Elizabeth's head was visible.

"It appears your father did not come home until the wee hours. He immediately bathed and departed again. His valet, Carstairs, has indicated that Mr. George Darcy will be gone at least two days."

Elizabeth's head tilted. "I am surprised the man is not more loyal to his employer. What is he thinking to repeat information so freely?"

Smith hummed and lifted up on his heels briefly. "Oh, he does not come right out and tell me. Generally, Carstairs has revealed things before he realizes that he has."

When Darcy chuckled, Elizabeth looked up at him, her eyebrows drawn together. He looked down at her with a grin. "Smith is very clever. He has a way of asking questions in a roundabout manner that Carstairs never sees coming."

"How interesting. And, is he not clever enough to figure this out for himself?"

Smith cleared his throat. "I believe he always figures it out after the fact. When I see him next, he will glare at me quite fiercely. However, in the future, he will have either forgotten or been distracted or something and it will happen again."

"He is not the most intelligent of people," Darcy murmured wryly. "Elderly and blindly loyal, but not very smart."

"Oh, I see."

Darcy hugged her close. "Shall we break our fast up here, then, my love?"

"Yes, that would be lovely." Elizabeth yawned. "I may need a nap afterwards."

"You would not wish to do too much too soon, madam." Smith gestured toward the dressing room. "If you like, I will have Jenny arrange a bath and help you dress while I call for breakfast."

"I bathed last night. I think I will be fine today." Elizabeth looked up into Darcy's face. "Would you rather dress first?"

"No, I see Smith has brought the newssheet up. I will read that while I wait for you. You go on ahead." Darcy looked at his valet and tipped his head toward the door. Once the servant had bowed and obeyed the silent command to leave, Darcy helped Elizabeth out of bed and into the dressing room, leaving her in the capable hands of her maid.

Hours later, after the couple had completed their morning ablutions, broken their fast, and napped, they sat in front of the fireplace in the wingback chairs arranged there for that purpose. It was too warm for more than a low-burning fire, and that only at Darcy's insistence that Elizabeth not become chilled again, but the atmosphere of the arrangement suited them, and so they pulled the chairs close and read to each other and talked.

A knock on the hallway door startled them. Darcy began to rise to open it when Smith hurried in from the dressing room, where he and Jenny had been working on repairs to clothing and polishing boots. The valet had a quick word with the servant in the hall, then sent the person off and closed the door. He approached the fireplace and bowed.

"Who was it?" Darcy tilted his head to the side.

"Mr. Baxter. He said Lord and Lady Matlock are in the formal parlor with Colonel Fitzwilliam, and they wish to speak to you and Mrs. Darcy."

Chapter 15

"My aunt and uncle are here, and without an invitation?" Darcy's brows creased. "That is unusual." He turned to Elizabeth. "It must be on account of you, my love. They wish to meet you."

Elizabeth's brows shot up to nearly her hairline. "They wish to meet me so badly that they would arrive unannounced, less than a day after we get to town?"

Darcy lifted and dropped his shoulders. "That is the only reason I can come up with. Do you feel well enough to go down and meet them?"

"I suppose I do." Elizabeth waited for Darcy to dismiss Smith and stand. "What should I know about them?"

"They are rather formal." Darcy held his hand out to assist her up. "I have never been close with them, though Richard and I are friends." He paused, his focus seemingly on tucking Elizabeth's hand into the crook of his elbow. "They have joined with my father in rebuking me more than once for my supposed bad and ungrateful behavior." He shook his head. "Richard says he talks me up to them, but I have not seen where that has made a difference. I suggest we be cautious with them, as we have with others, so that nothing untoward gets back to my father."

Elizabeth nodded. "That is what we will do. We will be formal with each other, as well?" When Darcy nodded, she smiled up at him. "Lead on."

They were silent as Darcy escorted Elizabeth down the stairs. She let go of his arm at the bottom of the staircase and straightened her skirt. He led her to the room holding his relatives and nodded to the footman to open the door and announce them.

Inside the room, a smiling young man in a brand-new horse guards uniform, carrying the insignia of a colonel, stood near an older couple dressed in the latest fashions. Darcy halted a few steps in, his wife following suit, and bowed. "Lord Matlock, Lady Matlock, Fitzwilliam. What a surprise it was to hear you had stopped by to see us."

"Good afternoon, Nephew." Lord Matlock tipped his head at Darcy. "You father informed us of your marriage. Your aunt insisted we come by immediately to meet your bride. Would you introduce us?"

"Certainly." Darcy held his hand out to Elizabeth, who placed her fingers in his palm. "This is my wife, Elizabeth Darcy. Elizabeth, this gentleman is my uncle, Henry Fitzwilliam, Lord Matlock. Beside him is my aunt, Audra Fitzwilliam, Lady Matlock. On the other side of her, the rogue with the grin is my cousin, Colonel Richard Fitzwilliam."

Richard bowed. "Welcome to the family, Mrs. Darcy. Has my cousin treated you well, or shall I run him through with my new sabre?" He patted the handle of his weapon. He winked at Darcy, but the smile he gave Elizabeth was gentle and encouraging.

With a quick but perplexed glance at her husband, Elizabeth replied to Richard's tease. "Mr. Darcy has treated me very well, but I thank you for your gallant offer." The corners of her lips twitched as she struggled valiantly to remain composed.

Darcy cleared his throat, raising a single brow at his cousin. "Thank you for defending me, Mrs. Darcy. Cousin, perhaps you should learn how to use that weapon before you make threats you cannot follow through with."

Richard looked startled for a moment, but then threw his head back and laughed. "Perhaps I should." He flung an arm around Darcy's shoulders. "How have you been?"

"I am well." When his cousin gave him an earnest look, Darcy reaffirmed his words. "I promise. I am very well."

With a nod, Richard let Darcy go and stepped back to allow his mother to speak to Elizabeth.

Lady Matlock had been examining her new niece closely as the girl interacted with Richard and Darcy. "We are pleased to make your acquaintance, Mrs. Darcy. Mr. George Darcy did not tell us anything about you other than your father is a gentleman from Hertfordshire."

Lord Matlock nudged his wife with his elbow, giving her a wide-eyed look. "You will have to pardon my wife. Her curiosity leads her to forget her usual politeness."

Lady Matlock sniffed. "Indeed. I apologize to you both. I know better."

Elizabeth stared at her husband's aunt for a long moment before turning her gaze toward Darcy. She spoke not a word, but her pointed look roused him to action.

"Please, do be seated." Darcy gestured to the settee on which his aunt and uncle had previously been seated, then guided Elizabeth around to its mate on the other side of the seating area. When she was settled, he took his place beside her.

Richard, who had taken up a chair between the two couples, spoke next. "Mother was eager to greet you, but so were we all. My brother was unable to join us, but I am certain you will meet him soon."

Elizabeth stopped fussing with her skirts and looked at her new cousin. "I will be pleased to meet him, as I am you." She swiveled her head toward the earl and countess. "You, as well, Lord and Lady Matlock."

Lady Matlock sighed. "I fear we have gotten off on the wrong foot. We truly are pleased to meet you. I know that this marriage was arranged and that the pair of you did not meet until the wedding. I expressed my displeasure to my brother, but he would not be swayed." She shook her head. "I know it is rather untoward for us to suddenly appear on your doorstep, but it was important to us to convey our support, privately at least. I plan to host a ball in your honor very soon."

Elizabeth watched the countess as she spoke. The lady was formal in her manner, but her words were almost friendly. Still, without knowing how trustworthy she was, Elizabeth could only retain her caution. "Thank you, madam." She looked to Darcy, whose lips wore the ghost of a smile as he watched her. She kept her gaze focused on her husband as he spoke to his aunt.

"Thank you, Aunt. You know already that we must gain my father's permission to attend. He is away for a day or two, but I will make the request as soon as he returns."

Elizabeth turned her head toward the other couple just in time to catch Lord Matlock look at his wife and tip his head toward the door. The countess pressed her lips together for a brief moment as she glanced out into the hallway. Elizabeth stopped herself from turning to see what had caused the interaction. It would not do to display too much curiosity at this point.

"The pair of you will come for tea this afternoon." Lady Matlock's pronouncement was accompanied by her move to stand. The rest of the party rose with her. "We expect you at six."

Darcy sputtered but finally agreed. He and Elizabeth saw their guests to the door and, when the panel had shut behind them, silently re-entered the parlor, shutting and locking the doors. They moved into the center of the room and stood, facing each other, holding hands.

"Do you feel well enough to go?" Darcy's thumb rubbed his wife's knuckles.

"I confess I am tired at the moment, but if I rest a while, I should be able to manage tea at six." Elizabeth paused. "That was a strange interview, did you not think?"

"I did." Darcy shrugged. "I am not as familiar with Lord and Lady Matlock as I am with Richard, but they did not seem anything but sincere."

"I agree. They did appear to be genuine. I thought your aunt was an odd combination of cold formality and warm welcome, if that makes sense. Her manner was correct, almost painfully so, but her words had a warmth to them that did not match her demeanor."

"Let us hope they end up being open and honest, and faithful to the son of their sister and his wife." Darcy looked down. "It would be nice to have another ally to defend me – us – to my father. Richard is, to a point, but he can only do so much."

Elizabeth nodded thoughtfully. "I hope it turns out well." She yawned, a twinge in her sore throat making her wince. "May we retire to our rooms now? I would dearly love a nap; unless, of course, you would like to do something else while I sleep."

Darcy had noted Elizabeth's grimace. He pulled her close, wrapping his arms around her back. "I will have some willow bark made up for you. I would give you whiskey and honey, but you need to be awake and alert for tea." He caressed her cheek. "I will always prefer being with you to any other activity." He bent his head and pressed his lips to hers for a brief kiss, then led her to the door.

<div align="center">~~~***~~~</div>

Darcy and Elizabeth chose to walk to Matlock House, which was across the square from the Darcy residence. They knocked on the door at precisely six o'clock. Within moments, they were announced to the residents.

"Welcome!" Lord Matlock strode forward, shaking Darcy's hand and kissing Elizabeth's. "Come; I must introduce Tansley to you." He gestured the young couple to precede him to the center of the room, where the colonel stood with another gentleman. "Son, this is Mrs. Elizabeth Darcy. Mrs. Darcy, this is my heir, Trevor Fitzwilliam, Viscount Tansley."

Elizabeth curtseyed. "It is a pleasure to meet you, sir."

Tansley took Elizabeth's hand and bowed over it. "The pleasure is all mine, Mrs. Darcy." He straightened, shaking his cousin's hand. "Very well done, even if you had no choice in the matter. She is lovely."

Darcy flushed, both from embarrassment and aggravation. "Thank you. She is."

Richard prevented his brother from saying anything more to distress their cousin. "Come, Mrs. Darcy, and sit down. Mother should be returning soon; she had to settle something with a couple of the maids." He took Elizabeth's hand and placed it on his arm, then moved them toward the grouping of couches and chairs at one end of the room, glancing over his shoulder to make sure Darcy followed. "There you are." He assisted his new cousin as she sat. "Sit next to her, Darcy. Tansley, you take that chair over there and I will sit here. Mother and Father can sit over there." By the time he had everyone arranged to his satisfaction, Lady Matlock had returned to the drawing room.

"Good afternoon, Darcy, Mrs. Darcy." The countess accepted the greetings of her guests and waved them back down. "I am so pleased you are here. The tea should be here shortly." She settled her skirts around her and looked up as her husband sat beside her. "Have you introduced our niece to Tansley?"

"I did." Lord Matlock patted his wife's arm. "I told you I would not forget."

"Hmm." Lady Matlock twisted her lips into a frown for a brief moment before lifting her eyes to heaven and turning her attention back to her sons and visitors. She opened her mouth to speak, but a maid came through the door with the tea service, so she shut it until the servant had left the room, pulling the wooden panel closed behind her.

"I will lock the doors." The earl's quiet murmur earned him a nod from his countess, who immediately began to prepare the tea pot.

"I apologize again for what must seem as strange behavior on our part." Lady Matlock rested her hands in her lap while the tea steeped. "My husband and I have come to be aware of the manner in which things are allowed to proceed at Darcy House; we wished for more privacy to speak with you than we felt we had there, so we came up with this invitation as a way to get you here."

Darcy and Elizabeth sat stiffly, their gazes fixed upon his aunt. Neither spoke.

"All is well, Darcy." Richard leaned forward, speaking urgently. "I told you I had spoken to my parents often, praising you. When they discovered your father's stubborn refusal in regards to your marriage, they came to me for answers. I believe they understand now what I tried so often to tell them, that you were not ungrateful and rebellious but were instead a victim."

Chapter 16

Darcy's brow creased. He darted a look at his aunt and uncle before turning his eyes back to Richard. "They believe you? You are certain?" When his cousin nodded, Darcy asked it again. "They do not think I am nothing but a wild and disobedient boy?"

"No." Richard shook his head. "They do not." He gestured to his parents. "Ask them."

Darcy moved his intense stare from his friend to his uncle and aunt. "This is true?"

Lord Matlock nodded. "It is, and I am so sorry we did not investigate a little further before we chastised you. I knew when my sister married George Darcy that he could be a hard man, but he had softened while she was alive and I did not realize how far backwards he had gone."

Lady Matlock, dabbing the corners of her eyes with a handkerchief, made her own plea. "If we had realized, we would never have allowed him to continue. We would have persuaded him to permit you and Georgiana to come to us, at least part of the year. Can you forgive us?"

"You will not be informing my father of every word I have said here?" Darcy remained stiff, his countenance blank, his jaw clenching.

The earl and countess shook their heads. "No," Lord Matlock said. "We will never tell him anything again, nor will we listen to his tales. You are my sister's only son. I would have you treated the way she wanted you to be, with love and gentle guidance."

The six sat in silence as Darcy and Elizabeth processed his uncle's words. Darcy was torn. Part of him wished to embrace this opportunity, to believe it and immerse himself in his mother's family. Another part of him, the part that had been treated harshly for so long, was afraid to trust mere words. He was beginning to develop a headache from it all when he felt Elizabeth slip her small hand into his. Remembering that he had more than himself to think about now, and relishing the calm peace her touch afforded him, he turned his head to look at her. "What do you think?"

"I think you should trust them. Your cousin has been your friend for a long time and I know you trust him. He says they have seen the light, they say they have seen it." Elizabeth shrugged. "It is your decision, but I confess it would be a relief to me to know there was someone with whom we could relax a bit."

Darcy nodded, unconsciously twining his fingers with his wife's. "Very well. Thank you."

He lifted Elizabeth's hand and kissed the fingers, then lowered it to his thigh, where he retained his grip on it. He looked at his relatives and nodded. "I accept your apology." He indicated the viscount. "What does Tansley think about it?"

The viscount leaned forward. "I am in agreement with Mother and Father, and I also apologize for not believing you when you proclaimed your innocence. I am sorry."

"You are forgiven." Darcy swallowed, emotion rising up inside him. "Thank you, all of you, for this. As my wife has said, it is a huge relief to feel, well, not alone."

The group was silent for a minute or two as they worked to keep their composure. Then, Lady Matlock began to pour out cups of tea, handing them to her husband to pass around. Once everyone was settled with a cup and some cake, she began to speak. "We must introduce you to society, Mrs.-" She lowered her plate to her lap. "I cannot continue to call you Mrs. Darcy in the family party, and you must not call me Lady Matlock. Please, do call me Aunt Audra, as Darcy does."

"Thank you … Aunt Audra." Elizabeth stumbled a bit over the name. "You may call me Elizabeth, or Lizzy, if you prefer. My sisters call me Lizzy."

"Excellent, Elizabeth." The countess took a bite of cake and set the plate aside. She picked up her cup, taking a sip, then lowering it to her lap. "I mentioned a ball earlier. I am planning it for the last Tuesday of the month. It will be a presentation of sorts for you, as well as an acknowledgement of your marriage. "Have you a ball gown?"

"Yes, I do. The dressmaker in Lambton made it for me. I have not had opportunity to wear it yet."

Lady Matlock nodded. "Mrs. Parker is an excellent seamstress. My sister used her often." She paused. "You only had one made?"

"One ball gown, yes." Elizabeth lifted her shoulders. "I had a riding habit made and two day dresses." She blushed and glanced at her husband. "My funds were limited; I had to be selective in what I chose."

Darcy also turned red. "My father has decreed that Elizabeth's pin money must cover her clothing in addition to anything else she needs. He will not be budged on the matter." He scowled at his cup.

"Well, that will not do!" The countess turned to her husband. "We must make him do this for her. Four gowns are not near enough for the season in town."

"We will, I promise you." The earl leaned back in his seat, a thoughtful look on his face. "We cannot let on that we know the situation, lest trouble fall on our nephew and niece because of it. Give me a day or two to think about how to approach it. If need be, I will offer to pay the bill myself."

Lady Matlock harrumphed. "Perhaps we should simply begin with that." She turned her attention back to Elizabeth. "We wished to invite you to the theater next week, but unless your ball gown is floor length, we will have to put it off. I shall make an appointment with my modiste for this coming week and have some things made up for you." She paused to think. "Perhaps she will have something already created that she can alter quickly, so you have an evening gown, as well."

Elizabeth did not quite know what to say, so she simply nodded and murmured a thank you.

The remainder of the visit was spent in conversation, with Elizabeth's background being reported to the Matlocks and a plan formulated to approach George Darcy about a wardrobe for her.

~~~***~~~
~~~

Two days later, the Darcy patriarch returned to London. His first order of business was to interrogate his new daughter's maid.

Jenny had been cleaning up the dressing room when Smith appeared.

"The master wishes to see you in his study." The valet looked grim.

Jenny put her hand to her bosom. "Oh, my. I had hoped to evade his notice."

"We have practiced this. You know how to reply, no matter what he does or says. You will not lose your position; you are paid out of Mrs. Darcy's pin money and it is she who says you stay or go. You are a quick thinker. You will be fine." Smith did his best to reassure her. Then, he nodded toward the door. "Go now, before he becomes angry at the delay. I will inform Mr. and Mrs. Darcy."

With a brisk nod, Jenny ducked her head and hurried out the door.

Smith did as he said he would, and when the maid returned twenty minutes later, white faced and panting, Elizabeth and Darcy were there, waiting for her.

Elizabeth rushed to Jenny's side. "Are you well? Come; sit over here. William, can you bring her something to drink? Sherry or tea or something?"

By the time the maid was settled into a seat, Smith had produced a bottle of port and poured a little for each of them. Jenny sipped hers slowly, her hand shaking.

Elizabeth gave the girl a little time to calm, then repeated her questions. "What happened? Are you well?"

Jenny nodded. "I am well. He did just as Smith warned me he would. He wanted details about you and Mr. Darcy, and threatened my employment if I did not tell. When I continued to refuse, he grew angry. At one point, I thought he might hit me, but he did not."

"How did you reply? What words did you use?" Smith stood behind her chair.

"I said what you told me to; I said Mrs. Darcy appeared neither happy nor unhappy and that I could not determine if she liked Mr. Darcy or not. No matter what he asked, I said I did not know." Jenny lifted her chin. "I hope he understands now where my loyalty lies."

Smith patted her on the shoulder. "I hope so, too, but do not be surprised if he calls you down again at some point."

"You did very well, Jenny. Thank you for your allegiance." Elizabeth, who had knelt beside her maid's chair, patted the servant's hand. "I appreciate that."

"I am glad that is over. Even if he does call me down again, I am confident now that I can prevail." Jenny shivered. "He is a bad one, Mr. George Darcy is."

Darcy agreed. "He is, very much so." He hesitated. "I wish to express my thanks, also, for your protection of Mrs. Darcy's privacy, as well as my own."

Jenny nodded in acknowledgement but said nothing.

Smith cleared his throat. "It occurs to me that Jenny could, perhaps, benefit from a period of rest. Dealing with Mr. George Darcy is exhausting for one seasoned to it. For a novice, the rush of feeling can be quite overwhelming."

"Of course!" Elizabeth looked up at Darcy. When he nodded, she spoke to her maid. "Take a few hours this afternoon to relax. I should not need you until it is time to dress for dinner. Mr. Darcy may attend me at bedtime, if I require assistance. He will not mind; will you, Husband?"

Darcy smirked. "I will not."

Elizabeth shook her head and giggled. "There. It is settled. You may catch up on your other work tomorrow."

"I confess a long nap would do me good. I will return to help you dress for dinner. Thank you, madam."

Elizabeth waved her away. "I will see you later on." She stood once the maid had exited the room. Then, she approached her husband. When he opened his arms, she stepped into the circle of his embrace, wrapping hers around his waist and laying her head on his chest. "Will he interrogate me, as well?"

"He could." Darcy chewed the corner of his lip as he thought. "I should have had you practice responses, the way Smith had Jenny practice."

Elizabeth shrugged. "I do not think it will matter. I am usually quick-witted. He does not frighten me. He disgusts me, but he does not scare me."

Darcy rubbed his hands over Elizabeth's back. "I am glad to hear it. Frankly, I am often frightened of him." He sighed. "I fear you have simply not had to deal with him often enough for it to scare you. I hate that it might ever happen."

Elizabeth squeezed her husband's waist. "I refuse to worry about the future. We are no longer alone. We will have to face him this evening, though."

Darcy sighed. "Unfortunately, we will." He was silent for several minutes, enjoying the feel of Elizabeth in his arms while at the same time, his mind raced ahead to what was certain to be an ugly dinner with his father. "I say we enjoy the next couple hours and prepare our spirits for the battle to come." He lifted her chin with his finger. "What say you?" He kissed her deeply, leaving them both breathless.

"I agree." Elizabeth's soft whisper led to more kisses and soon all thoughts of George Darcy were erased from their minds.

~~~***~~~

A half-hour before dinner, Darcy and Elizabeth descended the staircase arm in arm. As they usually did, they separated at the bottom, walking side by side to the drawing room.

"He is not here." Elizabeth looked around in surprise. "I thought he would be waiting for us."

Darcy put his hand at the small of his wife's back and escorted her to a seat. "He is unpredictable. He often commands me to do something or be somewhere to wait for him, only to fail to appear. He likes to keep those around him in suspense, I think."

Elizabeth sat on the couch, patting the seat beside her. "Well, since he is not here, come sit by me and tell me what you think your father will say to us."

Darcy obeyed with a short bark of laughter. "The first thing will likely be an inquiry as to pregnancy and a reminder of my inheritance."
~~~

"I am sorry. We *are* trying, though." Elizabeth placed her hand over his, which rested on his thigh.

"That we are." Darcy winked. After a quick glance out the doorway, he leaned in for a lingering kiss. He grinned when Elizabeth giggled.

"I plan to ask if we can visit my Aunt and Uncle Gardiner." Elizabeth looked down. "I would like to know why they supported my father in his scheme."

Darcy hesitated. "I do not wish for you to be disappointed if he refuses. My father is not one to agree to anything he thinks is not his idea, and he may very well carry negative feelings toward your uncle for not simply handing him the money he requested."

"I know." Elizabeth sighed. "I honestly do not think I truly wish to visit them, per se. I only want to garner my uncle's side of the story. I may well have to forgive him and my aunt for it without understanding." She shrugged. "I do not know, but I am prepared for him to deny my request."

They spoke a few minutes further about other things. Then, the dinner gong sounded and they rose and went through the door and into the dining room. Moments later, George Darcy entered from the hallway. "Sit down, already. I am starving and have no desire to wait for dawdlers." He strode to the head of the table and seated himself without waiting for the younger couple.

With lips pressed together, both Darcy and Elizabeth obeyed. Darcy sat Elizabeth at his father's left hand where the place settings had been laid out. He then moved around the table and sat at George Darcy's right. He glanced at the other end of the table with longing.

The first part of the meal progressed in silence. George was too busy eating to pay attention to his son and daughter-in-law, and neither of them wished to draw his attention, instead choosing to remain silent. Eventually, though, the older man's hunger was sated and he began to watch the other two.

"So, boy, have you done your duty yet? Is the chit with child?" George leaned back in his chair with his wine glass in hand.

Darcy flushed from his collar up. "It is too soon to tell."

"What do you mean, too soon? Has she had her courses? It has been nearly six weeks." George waved a servant forward to remove the plates and serve the second course.

Darcy gritted his teeth. "As I understand it, one cannot be certain of these things until the mother is well into the pregnancy. Six weeks is not enough time to know."

George snorted and turned to Elizabeth. "What, have you been using arts to keep from becoming in a family way, or are you simply unfertile? Surely that cannot be. You are one of five sisters." He laughed. "That would be a fine joke, would it not, Boy, if all your children were girls? No one to whom you could leave that inheritance you so crave."

Chapter 17

Elizabeth turned slitted eyes at her father-in-law. She opened her mouth to speak when she noticed, in her peripheral vision, her husband, shaking his head slightly. She moved her gaze back to him and, with a glare, looked down at her plate. Her father-in-law continued to speak disrespectfully to her, taunting her and his son, but she would not even look at him. She held herself rigid and stiff, her jaw clenched tightly and her hands twisted together in her lap.

George snorted. "Too good to speak, eh? Thought you might be. I do not know why, when you have the connections you do. Stupid chit."

Darcy carefully set his fork and knife on his plate. He took a deep breath and then turned to George. "Mrs. Darcy is a lady, Father. Do not speak to her that way."

George's countenance turned a deep red. His arm shot out, the back of his hand connecting with his son's cheek. "Do not tell me what to say, Boy!" He jumped up, fists clenched at his side.

The blow to Darcy's face knocked him off balance, and he started to fall over. The chair, which like all the furniture in this room had rather thin, spindly legs, broke, sending him to the floor.

Elizabeth had lifted her head when she heard her husband defend her. She witnessed the blow, but before she could do more than blink, Darcy was falling. "William!" She leaped from her seat and rushed around the table to kneel at his side. Seeing his lip bleeding, she snatched his napkin off the floor beside him, pressing it to the wound. Her eyes met her husband's. "Are you well?"

All Darcy could do was nod and grab her hand, squeezing it hard to communicate with her to remain quiet. There was no point in speaking; George had begun screaming obscenities and threats at them.

"Get out of my sight!"

At his father's final statement, Darcy scrambled backwards, out of reach of his father's boots and fists, and to his feet, grabbing Elizabeth's hand and dragging her out the door with him. His instinct was to do what he had always done: run. Get out of his father's way and to his rooms, where he was reasonably certain he could remain safe. He could feel his cheek and lip swelling as he rounded the banister and started up the staircase.

Elizabeth followed without a word. She clung to Darcy's hand, lifting her skirts with the other so she would not trip over them. Silently, they climbed and, reaching the third floor, hastened down the hall and into their rooms, locking the door behind them.

Smith appeared, emerging from the dressing room. "I heard your father from the kitchens and came up straight away." He approached, wincing when he saw the rapidly darkening bruise. "I will go down and see what I can find to reduce the swelling. Ice or a steak would do, but I may not be able to access either of them."

"Witch hazel will work, if you cannot get ice." Elizabeth led Darcy to a chair.

Smith bowed slightly. "I will look for some."

Darcy leaned his head against the back of the chair with a groan. He waved his hand in Smith's direction, and the valet bowed again and spun, going back through the dressing room. He heard the man tell Jenny to lock the door behind him and closed his eyes.

Elizabeth, having seen her husband settled and with nothing to occupy her hands or mind while they waited for Smith to return, began to pace up and down the room. "I cannot believe what just happened! How can a father treat a son so?" She stopped speaking to look at Darcy, but never broke her stride. "How? It is unnatural! He was so, so …" She waved her hand in the air. "So violent!" Suddenly, she stopped, turning first white and then green, and spun on her heel. She raced into the dressing room.

Darcy had opened his eyes and watched Elizabeth pace as best he could, given that his swollen cheek was impeding his sight in one of them. He saw her change colors and started to ask if she was well, but stopped when she turned and ran. He jumped up from the chair and followed her, losing his balance at first and bouncing off the post on the corner of the bed. When he arrived in the dressing room, Elizabeth was on her knees in front of the toilet chair, spewing the contents of her stomach into the chamber pot therein. He knelt beside her, demanding a damp cloth from Jenny, who had frozen in place at the sight of her mistress speeding into the room.

Darcy wrapped an arm around his wife's shoulders, murmuring soothing words into her ear. She sobbed, crying harder each time her stomach spasmed. He accepted the wet cloth from Jenny and used it to wipe Elizabeth's forehead and cheeks. Soon, the heaving stopped and she slumped into his arms. He held her close, kissing her head and whispering words of love.

"I am sorry." Elizabeth sniffed. "I do not know what happened."

Darcy ran his hand up and down his wife's back. "You witnessed something appalling. Chilling, even. It is no surprise that it upset you to the point of illness."

Elizabeth shuddered. "It was all I could do to remain quiet. That man needs taken down a peg."

Darcy leaned his uninjured cheek on Elizabeth's head. "He does." He sighed. "Would that I was strong enough to be the one to do it."

"I am. Allow me to tell him, William."

"No. Such an action would put you in danger. Surely you can see that he does not care who he hurts or how. Your status as my wife and a female would not stop him." Darcy tightened his grip on Elizabeth, who was quiet for a long time after he stopped speaking.

Eventually, recovered enough to become uncomfortable sitting on the floor, Elizabeth rose. Darcy stood with her and together, they moved back into the bedroom. Darcy sat in the chair again, this time pulling his wife into his lap. They sat in silence, deep in their own thoughts.

When Smith returned, a towel and a bowl of ice chips in his hand, Elizabeth would have risen, but Darcy tightened his grip. His whispered plea for her to stay was met with a blush and a nod. He drew comfort from having her near and suspected she needed the closeness, as well.

That night, as Elizabeth rested in his arms, the events at dinner replayed themselves in Darcy's mind. He felt again the fear, for himself as usual, but also for his wife. Frustration accompanied the usual anger that followed closely on the heels of anxiety. "What can I do? Elizabeth should not be exposed to such violence any more than Georgiana should, but I cannot send her even to Matlock House except during the day. If she were already with child, I would not hesitate."

Darcy checked to make sure his whispered words had not caused Elizabeth to wake up. He was relieved to see that she slept on. He kissed her ear and held her closer as his thoughts began to wander again. I need to find some fortitude and stand up to him. I should have been more forceful. The memory of the blow to his cheek and the humiliation and pain that accompanied it filled his mind, making the contusion that covered him from jaw to eye ache. He sighed. What would have happened had I done that? I may have gotten worse, and Elizabeth would surely have been caught up in it. My lovely, brave wife. Darcy kissed her hair. I would have had to hit him back. Could I do that? I have dreamed of doing so since I was a child, but the reality of the situation has always kept me from fulfilling that desire. He thought about what he learned in church about honoring his parents. How can I honor him if I am stooping to his level?

Darcy's thoughts circled in a similar manner half the night. He hated that he appeared as less of a man in front of Elizabeth, but had no experience with any other reactions. Finally, exhausted and in pain, he decided to speak to his uncle about it all. He fell into a deep but restless sleep.

~~~***~~~

Wednesday arrived, and with it the day Elizabeth was supposed to visit the modiste with Lady Matlock. Meals since Monday's dinner had been silent, so she did not know if the earl and countess had spoken to George or not. Darcy was unable to tell her. As usual after an outburst, his father had ignored him. Smith, usually a fount of details, could not say, either. She told her husband, "I decided to dress as though I am going. If he makes a fuss, it is easy enough to change my gown."

Darcy kissed her as he pulled her into his arms. "That is a very sensible plan. I will endeavor to find out for certain." He smiled down at her. "I would like to go with you, at least to Mat-
~~~

lock House. I would like to discuss what happened with my uncle."

Elizabeth stroked Darcy's uninjured cheek. "I think that is an excellent idea. Perhaps he can help us somehow."

"Perhaps." Darcy kissed her again, slow and deep. Then, with a sigh, he lifted his head. "We should go down."

Elizabeth stood on tiptoe to press a quick kiss to his lips. "Yes, let us get this over with." She took Darcy's arm and walked with him into the hall and toward the stairs. She stopped him at the top, before they began to descend. "I love you, William. The situation we are in is awful, but being a victim of such violence does not make you any less a gentleman." She paused and blushed. "I do not know why I chose to say that here, but I suspect you needed to hear it."

A soft smile spread across Darcy's mien as he looked down at his wife. "Thank you. I did need to hear it." He leaned down to whisper into her ear. "If we were not required at breakfast, I would show you just how much I needed it." He pulled his head back and chuckled when her blush deepened.

When they arrived at the dining room, George was already eating. He had nothing to say, keeping his eyes on the newspaper at his left hand, as they filled their plates from the spread on the sideboard and moved to the table to sit side by side. All three ate in silence, which was only broken when the elder Darcy stood from the table.

"Matlock informs me the countess insists on taking you shopping. He has convinced me to pay the bill and to allow you, Boy, to accompany him while the ladies shop. Do not give me reason to regret allowing these things." George slapped the table, picked up his newssheet, and strode out of the room.

Darcy and Elizabeth both sighed in relief. "Shall we eat quickly and go to my uncle's house right away?"

"Yes, let us do that." Elizabeth immediately turned her attention to her plate.

Within a quarter hour, the couple had completed their objective. The butler invited them into Matlock House, leading them to the dining room, where Lord and Lady Matlock were finishing their coffee. They were surprised to see two others sitting at the table with them. Before they could speak, Lady Matlock's shocked voice drew their attention.

"What happened to you?"

Darcy looked down, redness creeping up from his neck. He forced himself not to lift his hand to touch his cheek. He could not think of a reply, and so remained silent.

"Darcy, tell us." Lord Matlock's deep voice demanded an answer.

Darcy felt Elizabeth draw in a breath and quickly reached for her hand, hoping to silence her.

The earl sighed. "Never mind. I suspect I know. I hope you do not still think we will take his side."

Darcy could not bring his head up. His eyes continued to examine the carpet in front of him. "No, sir, I do not."

"Has it been treated?" Lady Matlock exchanged a glance with her husband.

"Yes, it has." Elizabeth explained the treatment Smith had given it.

The countess unhappily eyed the large purple contusion. "Good. Nothing else can be done, I do not think." She paused and then changed the subject. "Go ahead and greet your cousin and aunt while I have the housekeeper lay two more places."

Darcy murmured his acceptance of Lady Matlock's instructions, then bowed a greeting to his other aunt. "Lady Catherine, I did not expect to see you." He looked at his hosts, uncertain about his next step.

"All is well, Darcy. She has been informed of the situation; she will not betray you."

"Indeed?" Darcy looked from Lord Matlock to Lady Catherine.

"Yes, indeed." Lady Catherine sniffed. "After the way he behaved with me yesterday, I never wish to see or speak to him again." She examined Elizabeth closely, drawing one corner of her lips down. "Who have you here?"

"This is my wife, Elizabeth. Elizabeth, this is my other aunt, Lady Catherine de Bourgh. She is my mother's sister." Darcy had placed his hand at the small of Elizabeth's back as he spoke. He kept it there, meaning it as a sign of possession and a warning of sorts.

Elizabeth curtsied. "I am pleased to make your acquaintance, Lady Catherine."

Darcy's aunt sniffed again. Then, she turned to her left. "This is my daughter, Miss Anne de Bourgh. She was named for my sister."

Elizabeth and Anne greeted each other with curtseys and smiles.

"What brings you to town?" Darcy suspected he knew the answer to his question, but wished to hear it from his aunt.

Lady Catherine shot a look at her brother. "I made a visit to Darcy House yesterday."

"You did?" Darcy's eyes grew wide. He glanced at Elizabeth, noting her confusion. "We were not made aware of it or we would have come down to greet you."

With a pointed look at the deep purple, slightly swollen bruise on her nephew's face, Lady Catherine made her sentiments known. "I was not there long. I was abused most horribly for my temerity in objecting to your marriage."

"You objected to our marriage?" Elizabeth's eyebrows drew together. "I suppose I should not be surprised, given the circumstances of it, but I have not heard much about you from William, so I had not supposed you to be close enough that you would."

Lady Catherine sniffed. "I reminded George Darcy of my sister's wish for her son to marry my daughter. However, after hearing the things he said to me, I have changed my mind. Even if it were possible for your marriage to be set aside, I would not want my delicate Anne to be subject to that ungentlemanly, monstrous, domineering reprobate." She paused, her chin quivering. "My sister would be ashamed to know her precious George had turned into such an awful man."

Lady Matlock's eyes filled with tears. She leaned forward. "She would be." The countess sat back, blinking her eyes and resuming her stiff posture.

The occupants of the room sat without speaking for several minutes. Lord Matlock was the first to break the silence. "We must not lose ourselves in thoughts of the dead when we have the living to deal with. Sister, I suggest you go home and plan a debut for your daughter. You knew all along that Anne was not serious about a marriage between the children. She was speculating; that is all. You should be grateful for it, I think." He turned to his wife. "My lady, I believe you and our niece have an appointment with Madam Claire today."

"We do." Lady Matlock looked at Anne and Lady Catherine. "Would you ladies like to go with us?"

Lady Catherine answered. "No, I do not think we will. My brother is correct; I need to plan for Anne to debut next season. At eighteen, she will have just as good a chance as anyone at making a match."

"Very well. If you change your mind, Madam Claire is in Bond Street." The countess rose. "It was good to see you both, even if the circumstances were not what we would have wished for." She walked around the table to her niece and sister, who had risen upon her approach.

She hugged each of them briefly. "Have a safe trip home, and do not wait so long to come back and visit again."

Chapter 18

That afternoon, Darcy and Elizabeth returned to Darcy House, tired but happy. They took tea in their rooms and discussed their day.

"What did you purchase?"

Elizabeth rolled her eyes. "Half the silk in London, I venture." She chuckled along with Darcy. "Aunt Audra had me outfitted with multiple gowns for every possible occasion. Ball gowns, gowns for the theater, morning dresses, nightshifts, gowns to wear for dinner parties, and all the underpinnings to go with each. Madam Claire said the bulk of the order would be delivered in a fortnight, but I do not see how that many items could be completed in that length of time." She shook her head.

Darcy smiled and picked up her hand. "I noticed a footman carrying boxes up the stairs."

"Ah, yes. Those would contain a few things to get me through the next week. The modiste had an order cancelled recently, so there were several gowns already completed that only needed a tuck here and there to fit me perfectly. One of the boxes contains a gown for the theater next week, assuming your father allows us to go. Would you like to see it?" Elizabeth rose and headed for the dressing room without waiting for her husband's reply.

"I would, yes." Darcy called after her. He laughed softly and shook his head. It was clear to him that Elizabeth was excited about this dress. He absently reached for a cake and ate it while he waited, his mind drifting to today's conversation with the earl. He was brought back to the present when she rushed back into the room, holding a gown up to her front.

"What do you think? I did not put it on because I did not wish to tear it. Is it not the loveliest shade of lilac?" Elizabeth smiled happily into his eyes.

"Yes, it is." Darcy tipped his head. "It does something to your eyes. It gives the brown a slight purple tint." He squinted as he looked more closely at her irises. "Perhaps that is just a reflection of the gown." He laughed when she stomped her foot and growled at him. "It is a gorgeous dress and the color becomes you very well. I shall be immeasurably proud to enter the theater with you on my arm."

Elizabeth stopped, the gown clutched to her chest. "Truly?"

"Truly, my love." He grinned when she leaned down to kiss his cheek.

"Thank you. You are the best of men." She whirled away. "Give me a moment to put this away and then you can tell me about your day."

Darcy freshened the tea in both cups, and by the time the task was complete, Elizabeth had returned.

"Did you talk to your uncle?"

Darcy smirked. "Wasting no time, are we?"

"No, we are not." Elizabeth popped a small cake in her mouth and leaned back, arms crossed.

With a chuckle, Darcy began to relate his conversation with Lord Matlock. "Uncle Henry agrees with me that, given our need to become parents, it is impractical for you to live with them. We already know that my father will not give permission for me to go to Matlock House. We expect him to begin to demand I attend him at his clubs; with the completion of my courses at University, he will likely find a way to use me to his own benefit." Though Darcy spoke impartially, inside he retained a great deal of hurt over this. He pushed it aside for the moment.

"I do not know if I like the sound of that." Elizabeth reached for another cake but stopped. She swallowed.

"I do not either, but Uncle Henry promised to do his best to steer Father away from me when he can." Darcy shrugged. "He cannot be with me all the time and he is not my father's keeper, but he has said he will do his best to keep his eye on the situation."

"Did you ask about Georgiana?" Elizabeth scooted back deeper into the chair and closed her eyes for a moment.

"I did. Uncle plans to ask Father to allow my sister to visit for a few weeks when we leave town at the end of the season. Uncle will have duties in Parliament, but Aunt and Tansley can go to Derbyshire ahead of him, retrieve Georgiana, and take her to Ravensblack Manor. This will remove her from Father's reach and give her better models of behavior."

"It will. What do you think your father will say? Is there anything we can do to promote the idea to him?"

Darcy lifted his shoulders and dropped them again. "I do not think we should get involved. If Father asks, we should by all means throw our support behind the idea, but to present it to him in any other way would be folly. I believe my uncle will be persuasive enough to convince Father to allow her visit." He paused. "We also talked about what happened here Monday evening." He lifted a hand to gingerly touch the bruise on his face. "I asked him what I should have done differently. He said something to me that I had never considered before."

Elizabeth tilted her head. "What was it?"

Darcy licked his lips. "I have told you that I feel obliged to honor him, Father, I mean, as the Church teaches." When he saw Elizabeth nod, he continued. "Uncle said that honoring him does not mean I cannot physically defend myself or you, or even Georgiana. There are other ways to show him honor. For example, I live in his house and therefore obey his rules."

"Yes, that makes sense. What else did he say?" Elizabeth shifted in her chair.

"He became impassioned while we spoke and said something that shocked me, but the more I think about it, the more I agree. He said that Father gave up his right to be honored when he began to abuse me, and that I owed him nothing." Darcy watched Elizabeth's expression as she absorbed this idea.

"Yes, I see his point. A father is not intended to treat his child meanly, to degrade and humiliate him. He should be lifting you up, teaching you right from wrong and how to treat your fellow man with respect and grace. George Darcy has not done that. In fact, he has done quite the opposite. Your uncle is correct. You owe him nothing." Elizabeth paused. "How does this affect your daily interactions with him?"

Darcy shook his head. "I will still treat him as I wish to be treated. I will not suddenly become rude. However, I feel as though this idea gives me permission, if you will, to do more than cower and run. If I feel the need to protect you or Georgiana, or even myself, and it causes a physical confrontation, I am allowed to strike back."

"That is brilliant!" Elizabeth smiled and reached for Darcy's hand. "I am proud of you."

Darcy squeezed his wife's fingers. "Thank you." He reached for a cake. "Would you like another?"

Elizabeth froze, her eyes glued to the delicacy Darcy indicated on the plate. "No, thank you. You can have it." She rose from the chair. "I will be right back. I … I need to use the necessary." She darted toward the dressing room.

Darcy's brows creased as he watched Elizabeth fly across the room. He listened for a moment, but did not hear anything untoward, so he shrugged and ate his cake.

Tuesday, the following week

"You will be the loveliest lady at the theater." Darcy slid his hands around Elizabeth's waist. "You are stunning."

"Thank you, William." Elizabeth leaned back and looked her husband up and down. "You look exceedingly well, yourself."

Darcy grinned and pulled her closer. "Do I?" He bent his neck, placing his lips at her ear. "How convenient." He ran his tongue over the shell, above the earring dangling from the lobe.

Elizabeth sighed and ran her hands over Darcy's chest. "Yes." She slid her palms up and into his hair, pulling his head down for a kiss.

Several long moments later, the couple separated, lips swollen and chests heaving. "I love you," they said in unison, then laughed. Smith appeared in the dressing room doorway.

"Yes?" Darcy looked at his valet over Elizabeth's head.

"Sir, your father is demanding your presence in the entry hall. He says it is nearly time to leave."

With a nod and a resigned sigh, Darcy dismissed the servant. He held his arm out to Elizabeth. "Are you ready?"

"I am." She slipped her hand up under his elbow.

As the couple reached the bottom of the stairs, George Darcy berated them. "It is about time you got down here. What were you waiting for, Christmas? We will be late and I will have to listen to Matlock whine like a little girl about it." He paused in his tirade as a maid brought their outerwear. "Get on with it and get in that coach," he demanded, snatching his own hat, gloves, and cane from the servant.

Darcy and Elizabeth complied, quickly exiting the house and entering the carriage. They sat on the forward-facing seat, close together, but with hands in their laps and spines stiff. George heaved himself inside and settled on the other seat of the equipage, rapping his walking stick on the roof. He eyed his son and daughter-in-law as though looking for something to criticize.

Elizabeth kept her eyes glued to the window, her fingers twisted tightly together. Darcy kept half an eye on his father; experience had taught him to remain alert at all times in the man's presence. The remainder of his attention alternated between his hands in his lap and the window at his side. He could feel Elizabeth's tension and wished he could relieve some of it. Alas, that was not possible at this point in time. *I will try to find a moment alone with her*, he thought. *Or, perhaps, we can sit in the back of* the box and hold hands, out of sight of prying eyes. Buoyed by this idea, he began to look forward to the evening's entertainment.

The carriage stopped a fair distance down the street from the theater entrance. Peering out into the street, Darcy could see a large crowd milling about in front of the doors. Every few minutes, the vehicles in the line would move forward, the ones nearest the entrance disgorging passengers before moving away. He looked toward Elizabeth, who had turned her head to look out over his shoulder. He lifted one corner of his lips just a bit when she glanced at him, pleased to see her follow suit. They remained silent, and when George shifted on the other side of the equipage, she swiftly turned her eyes back to her own window.

Darcy's relief was acute when the family carriage halted in front of the theater's entrance and a groom opened the door. He waited for his father to exit before descending and holding his hand out to Elizabeth. He tucked her fingers under his arm and hurried after his father, who had not waited for them but instead had begun pushing through the crowd and into the building.

"It is quite a crush, is it not?" Elizabeth's quiet words drifted up to Darcy's ears.

"It is. I am surprised, given how early we are." He paused. "I fear we may lose my father in this mass of people, but we are sitting with my aunt and uncle. As long as we can locate them, we should be fine."

Elizabeth looked around her, scanning the sea of faces. "Is that not your aunt, over there by the stairs?"

Darcy glanced down at Elizabeth and, seeing her tilt her head toward the right side of the staircase, followed her gaze. "Yes, that is Lady Matlock." He steered his wife around a large group of gentlemen and then another large group of both gentlemen and ladies, finally arriving at the spot where his relatives waited.

"Darcy!" Colonel Fitzwilliam was the first to see them. "I was concerned you would be unable to locate us in this crowd."

"We were uncertain we could find you." Darcy looked around at the other attendees. "I am surprised to see this many people this late in the season. I had thought most would be on their way to the country by now."

"In a normal year, they would." Lady Matlock inserted herself into the conversation. "However, they have all received invitations to our ball and have decided to wait to make the trip. No one wishes to miss out on meeting Mrs. Darcy." She took Elizabeth's hands and leaned in to kiss her cheek. "How are you, my dear?"

Elizabeth curtseyed, then returned the countess' kiss. "I am well. I am happy to be here with you."

Lady Matlock squeezed her niece's hands with an understanding look. She turned to Darcy, extending her hand for him to bow over as Lord Matlock and his sons greeted Elizabeth.

"Your father is here. We saw him for a moment, just long enough to greet him, and then he darted off to speak to someone." The earl shook his head as he spoke, then turned to his wife. "Have we been seen enough, or can we retire to our box?"

Chapter 19

Lady Matlock seemed to Darcy to be surprised for a brief moment, but quickly rallied. "Of course. The performance will begin soon. We should go up."

The party of six began to ascend the stairs. Darcy noticed Elizabeth looking around in wonder. He leaned down so she could hear him. "Have you not been here before?"

Elizabeth shook her head. "Not to this theater, and never abovestairs. My uncle took Jane and me once to a different playhouse, but we sat on the floor and not in a box."

"I have not attended many more plays than you have, but it has always been in a box." Darcy looked around. "This is quite elegantly decorated, do you not think?"

"It is. It is beautiful." Elizabeth smiled at Darcy.

"Enough chatter. Keep up." The harsh voice of George Darcy behind them startled both Darcy and his wife. They instantly ceased speaking, their gazes forward and their spines stiffening. They were not far behind the earl and countess but picked up their pace, so that when they arrived at the box, they were on the other couple's heels.

Once inside, the group chose seats and began to settle themselves for the performance. Their progress was interrupted by a steady influx of other attendees who wished to greet them.

One of these people was a tall, thin, young man with reddish-blond hair and a sunny smile. Darcy perked up when the gentleman entered the box. "Bingley! How good to see you." He bowed. "How have you been?"

"Fine as ever." Charles Bingley laughed. "The question is, how are you?"

Lady Matlock appeared at Elizabeth's side. "Darcy, will you introduce me to your friend?" She craned her neck to catch her husband's eye, and he immediately stepped around the viscount and two of his friends to come to her side.

"Of course." Darcy gestured toward Bingley. "Lady Matlock, Lord Matlock, Mrs. Darcy, please meet my friend from University, Charles Bingley. Bingley, please meet my aunt and uncle, Lord and Lady Matlock." He paused as Bingley bowed to the peers and they greeted him. "And this …" He drew Elizabeth closer. "… is my wife, Mrs. Elizabeth Darcy."

Bingley bowed to Elizabeth. "I am pleased to make your acquaintance, Mrs. Darcy." He turned to his friend. "I had heard you were married."

Lady Matlock assured Bingley of the family's favor toward the match. "We are delighted to welcome Mrs. Darcy to the fold." She smiled at Elizabeth. "We look forward to getting to know her better." She turned her attention back to Bingley. "I believe Darcy requested an invitation to our ball be sent to you and your family?"

"I received one, yes, thank you. My parents and I will be delighted to attend." Bingley bowed.

"Excellent." Lady Matlock clapped her hands together. "I was hoping you would. You are the only person my nephew requested we invite. I would have tried to persuade you to attend, had you declined."

The colonel, who had come up behind his mother as she spoke, interrupted. "She would have reminded you that she is a countess and you, a mere plebeian."

Lady Matlock narrowed her eyes at her son but ignored him. "Please excuse me. I must go greet Lady Cavendish. It has been a pleasure, Mr. Bingley." With a regal tilt of her head, she excused herself and glided to the door of the box.

"What are you still doing in town, Bingley? Where are you sitting?" Darcy was eager to visit with his friend for the few short minutes he suspected he had before the bell rang indicating the beginning of the performance.

"My parents have rented a box further down the hall. We have been in town most of the spring. My elder sister got married a week ago, so our time and attention was focused on that for a long time. Months of being told to do all manner of things, from winding ribbons to giving opinions on menu items." Bingley shivered. "Puts a man off of getting leg-shackled, it does."

Darcy chuckled. Having caught sight of Elizabeth rolling her eyes, he grinned. "Indeed. And, your younger sister?"

"Ah, Caroline." Bingley shook his head. "Caroline has been in school. She was quite put out to hear of your marriage." He turned to Elizabeth. "My sister met your husband at Christmastide the year before last and decided he was her future mate. Nothing anyone said could sway her."

Elizabeth's brows rose. "Indeed?" She glanced at Darcy, who shook his head. "Hopefully she will meet someone when she makes her debut."

Their banter halted as the gong was sounded.

"Oh!" Bingley exclaimed. "I must be going. It was good seeing you, Darcy, and meeting you, madam." Bingley bowed. "I will see you next week at the ball, if not before." He darted out the door and was gone.

Darcy and Elizabeth, at a harsh word from George, sat in the seats they had chosen at the back of the box.

There were two rows of seats in the chamber, with four chairs in each row. The boxes were separated from those on each side by a low wall. Curtains hung on each side that could be pulled to give those seated in the boxes a bit of privacy, but the Matlocks preferred to keep their box open.

By previous arrangement among the earl and countess and their sons, Lady Matlock and her husband took the seats in the front on the right. Tansley was across the narrow aisle, and behind him was the colonel. With Darcy and Elizabeth behind the earl and countess, George Darcy had to choose between two seats on the far left side of the box. He decided to take the place beside the viscount. The earl and countess looked around as the play began, noting with a nod that their niece and nephew were separated from their brother-in-law, just as they had wished.

Darcy and Elizabeth noticed that his father was as far away as he could get, but thought nothing of it. Darcy surreptitiously moved their chairs close together before he seated Elizabeth and took his place beside her. Once settled, he reached for her hand, leaning back in the chair and crossing his leg to hide the sign of affection as well as he could. He rubbed his thumb across the back of her hand, feeling the comfort fill him that her touch always brought.

At intermission, the viscount and his brother went out to get refreshments for everyone, while their parents, uncle, and cousins were inundated with more visitors and well-wishers.

Elizabeth happened to catch sight of her father-in-law at one point and was shocked speechless. George Darcy had smiled quite charmingly at one of the ladies and bowed with an elegance she had never witnessed before. She looked up at her husband, who stood beside her, with a question in her eyes.

Darcy had followed Elizabeth's line of sight and witnessed his father with the woman, whom he had heard referred to by his aunt as Lady Allen. He knew the lady was unmarried and believed her to be a widow. He wondered what the elder Darcy was up to. Looking back down at his wife, he spoke in a low tone. "I have never seen him in the presence of a lady who is not family." He shrugged. "I know he wishes to be seen by society in a good light. It is his reason for disparaging me to all he meets. It makes him appear to be a loving and long-suffering father."

Elizabeth rolled her eyes and scowled. "He is deceitful on top of being unnatural. Lovely." She sniffed.

Soon, Lady Allen left the box and George turned to look out over the crowd and into the other boxes. He appeared bored by what he saw. Just as the next act was about to begin, he suddenly came to attention, watching someone in a box on a lower level on the other side of the theater. He turned, stepped past Tansley to Lord Matlock, and leaned down to murmur in his brother's ear. When Matlock nodded, he moved toward Darcy.

"Your uncle will take you home. Mind you do nothing to embarrass me while I am out of your presence, or it will not go easy for you." With a glare at Darcy and then one for Elizabeth, he stepped out the door and into the corridor.

Darcy and Elizabeth looked at each other and shrugged. He leaned forward and tapped his uncle's shoulder. "What is happening?"

Matlock shook his head. "I do not know, but I suspect he has found another entertainment to occupy his time the rest of the night." He tipped his head toward the boxes across from them, where George could be seen bowing to a woman.

Darcy gave a slow nod. "He must have run down the stairs to get there so quickly. Perhaps Elizabeth and I can relax, then. Thank you." He patted Matlock's shoulder and leaned back. He whispered to Elizabeth. "Father will probably not be home until the early morning hours, if then." He leaned back in his seat and threw his arm over the back of her chair. "We can relax and enjoy the rest of the performance." He smiled as he pulled her closer.

For the rest of the evening, Darcy kept his arm in place, often using his fingers to draw lines and circles on his wife's arm. She leaned as close to him as she dared while still maintaining propriety.

In the Matlock carriage on the way home, Darcy and his relatives discussed the events of the evening.

"I was told that Uncle George left early, with Nelly Blevins." Tansley spoke into the darkness.

Lady Matlock gasped. "Has he returned to his former habits, then?"

"Who is Nelly Blevins?"

Darcy squeezed his wife's hand. "As I understand it, she is a courtesan."

Lord Matlock affirmed this. "Yes, she is. A popular one, from what I hear."

"Do you think he intends to set her up as his mistress, Father?" The viscount asked.

"I do not know," the earl replied with a sigh. "He may. It has been a while since he has had anyone under his protection."

"I am uncertain I wish to hear this," Darcy muttered.

"I am sorry." Lord Matlock sounded contrite. "It is the way of the world, sadly. I cannot imagine doing such a thing. I am kept very happy at home."

"I, as well." Darcy lifted Elizabeth's hand and kissed her fingers. "This may sound terrible, but if he is out until morning, our night will be easier."

"True," Elizabeth conceded, "but think of that poor woman. Is she in danger from him?"

"I do not know. I hope not, but then, I hoped you and Darcy would not, either, and you are." Lord Matlock's frustration was clear.

The carriage pulled to a stop at that moment, and the earl peered out the window at the sidewalk. "We must have reached Darcy House."

The door opened and a groom appeared. "Darcy House, sir."

"Just as I thought. Darcy, you and Elizabeth get some sleep and relax while you can. I will be in touch in a day or two."

"Thank you, Uncle." Darcy descended and helped his wife down. "Good night."

The Matlock carriage pulled away and Darcy led Elizabeth into the house and up the stairs. By mutual agreement, they held off any discussion, instead opting for their bed and sleep.

<div align="center">~~~***~~~</div>

One week to the day later, Darcy and his wife spent a lazy day in their rooms. George had been gone more than he was home and the young couple had taken to remaining in their chambers a large part of each day. They were just beginning to break their fast when Elizabeth suddenly bolted from the room. Brow creased, Darcy followed. Without a word, he held his wife as she emptied her stomach, then washed her face and hands and helped her up. After Jenny had handed her a toothbrush and tooth powder, and Elizabeth had rinsed her mouth, he helped her back into the bedchamber and made her stretch out on the bed.

"We need to talk."

Elizabeth opened her eyes, which she had closed upon lying down. "What about?"

"About you and whatever it is that makes you lose the contents of your stomach so frequently. I think we should call the doctor in and have you examined."

Elizabeth sighed. "I tried to hide my illness from you."

Darcy shook his head. "You did not succeed. I know it has not been every day, but in the last fortnight, you have done exactly what you did today at least a dozen times. I thought at first it was a reaction to my father's presence, but he has not been home more than every two days and then only long enough to attend to correspondence and have a meal. He has not even dined with us every day. It cannot be your nerves." A thought entered his mind and he tilted his head as he watched Elizabeth's eyes close again. "You have also been tired much of the time." He paused. "I hate to ask this for fear of sounding as crude as my father, but have you had your monthly ..." He gestured with his hand up and down her form. "Your woman thing. What do you call that?"

Elizabeth's eyes popped open when he began his question and then rolled at the end of it. "My courses?"

"Yes, those." Darcy sounded relieved. "Have you had them?"

Elizabeth thought back. Her brows drew together. She sat up. Slowly, she said, "Not since before our wedding." She looked at her husband, her eyes widening. "Do you think …?"

"Have you talked to Aunt Audra about it at all?" Darcy pulled her close.

Elizabeth shook her head. "No, the subject never came up. I was too embarrassed to broach it and she never said anything, so I did not, either."

"All we can do is wait, then, and educate ourselves." Darcy fell silent as he thought. "There are medical texts in the library at Pemberley. There may be some here, as well. If not, I will try to find one. I should like to know what will happen as you increase, and what further symptoms you might experience."

"And how to know for certain." Elizabeth draped her arms over Darcy's shoulders.

"Yes, that, too." He smirked. "We should ask my aunt. I will if you will not."

Elizabeth shook her head as a light blush started at her neck and moved upwards. "I will try to get her alone tonight." She stopped speaking as a thought entered her mind. "We do not have to tell your father until we know for certain, do we?"

Darcy thought a moment, looking past Elizabeth's shoulder as he absently played with a curl of hair that dangled near her neck. "We probably should, but I am of a mind to wait until we are one hundred percent sure." He chuckled when she grinned. "This pleases you, I see."

"It does. I like the thought of keeping something secret from him." Elizabeth looked down, suddenly shy.

Darcy lifted her chin with his finger. "I do, as well. Do not feel as though you are the only one with those reactions." He lifted his lips in a small smile.

Elizabeth returned his expression with one of her own. "Very well." She paused. "I love you."

Darcy's lips widened. "I love you, as well." He looked at the clock on the mantel. "How much time do we have?"

Elizabeth giggled. "Enough, I daresay."

Chapter 20

Darcy and Elizabeth descended the stairs together, in enough time that George would have no reason to rebuke them. While they waited for the elder man's summons, they wandered through the rooms on the ground floor, examining the artwork that covered the walls. Darcy pulled his pocket watch from its place and checked the time.

"Father will be down soon. We should use the water closet while we can."

"Yes, I agree." Elizabeth strolled alongside Darcy toward the small room tucked under the stairs at the back of the house. "Do you wish to go first, or shall I?"

Darcy opened the door to the room and bowed to his wife. "You go first." He winked. "I would hate for you to be rushed."

Elizabeth raised an eyebrow. "Are you suggesting I take too long at my toilette?"

Darcy smirked and lowered his head for a quick kiss. "Not at all." He gestured for Elizabeth to enter the room, patting her backside as she walked past. He chuckled when she gasped and spun, then shut the door behind her.

Elizabeth did not dawdle, and soon was joining him in the hallway. "Your turn, witling." She giggled as he clutched his chest in mock agony and smirked.

While Darcy completed his business in the closet, Elizabeth began to examine the painting that hung on the wall opposite the small room. She heard footsteps on the stairs but ignored them. Darcy House had many servants and they were always moving about the home as they performed their duties. She expected whoever it was to move silently past her and so was startled to be addressed.

"Well, who have we here?"

Elizabeth spun around, her hand over her heart. Seeing the person dressed in the clothes of a gentleman, she dropped her hand. "I am sorry. I do not believe we have been introduced?"

The stranger smirked. "We have not, but I can figure out easily enough who you are." His eyes raked her form. "My godfather told me you were a prime article. I have never known him to be wrong when it comes to females."

"Your godfather?" Elizabeth's tone was frosty. Though she was reasonably certain who this person was, she chose to behave as though she had not the first clue. "I am afraid I do not know who that would be." She lifted her chin. "I do not speak to strangers, sir. I must ask you to excuse me." She curtseyed and made to move past him. She was stopped when his arm shot out and his hand gripped her upper arm. "Unhand me."

The gentleman chuckled. "I think not. Old Darcy failed to tell me you were feisty." He jerked her closer. "I like my women spirited. It is no wonder he mentioned taking you from Fitzwilliam and giving you to me. Undoubtedly, Fitz would not have the first clue what to do with you." His free hand slipped around her waist, gripping it firmly. "I can assure you, I know exactly what I am about."

Elizabeth pushed at his chest. "Let me go!" She turned her head as he leaned his down. As a result, his attempted kiss grazed her ear. With her unhindered hand, she drew back a fist and tried to strike him, but the man was too quick, he let go of her waist and stopped the blow, twisting her arm down and behind her back as he did so. She cried out. Suddenly, he let her go.

Darcy had been washing his hands in the ewer when he heard his wife exclaim in pain. He rushed out of the room in time to see his father's favorite push Elizabeth against the far wall. A red haze descended over his vision and he surged forward. "Get off of her, you blackguard!"

Darcy pulled Wickham away from Elizabeth, spinning him around. He slammed his fist into Wickham's face, knocking the other man to the floor. He took a step toward the fallen man, his enemy for as long as he could remember, when Elizabeth appeared in front of him.

"William. Stop. It is not worth the trouble it will cause." She placed her hand on his chest as she pleaded with him.

Darcy turned his intense stare on his wife, drilling his gaze into hers. "You will always be worth any trouble."

"Thank you. If it is true, then please, do not lower yourself to their level." Elizabeth's voice was little more than a whisper, but it was fierce nonetheless. "For me."

Darcy stared a bit longer, but soon nodded. "Very well." He unclenched his fists, which had hung by his side. He stepped back, away from Wickham.

From his place on the floor, the other man sneered. "Giving me another thing to tell your father about, are you?" He rolled to his side, rubbing his jaw. "Surely you do not think I will keep this between us?"

"Tell him what you like. I do not care." Darcy pointed down the hall toward the front door. "I want you gone from this house immediately. You are never to enter again when Mrs. Darcy is in residence."

Wickham laughed. "You have no authority to say that."

Darcy's glare bore into the eyes of his nemesis. "As her husband, I do. If you do not leave immediately, I will remove you, myself."

"You are just jealous because *Mrs. Darcy* was showing attention to me." Wickham jeered. "You are not man enough to keep her focus. She will be mine soon enough, you wait and see."

Darcy growled and stepped toward the other man, fists clenched.

"What is going on here?" George Darcy pushed his way past his son and daughter-in-law and rushed to help Wickham off the floor. "What happened, George?" He turned accusatory eyes toward his son. "What did you do?"

Before Darcy could say anything, Wickham replied. "His wife threw herself at me and he attacked me."

George's lip curled. Ignoring Elizabeth's cry of protest and Darcy's roar of anger, he began to abuse them both while defending his favorite.

The red haze around Darcy, that had receded once Elizabeth spoke to him, rose up again to color everything he saw with its tint. "She did not throw herself at anyone. Wickham attacked her. I rescued her from his clutches. Look at her arm!" Darcy grabbed his wife and pulled her in front of him. "See that bruise? He twisted her limb behind her back and tried to assault her! I want him out of this house, and I want it now!"

For a moment, George looked taken aback, but he quickly rallied. "This is my house and I decide who stays and who goes."

Darcy moved closer to his father, ignoring Elizabeth, who tugged on his arm. "Mrs. Darcy is my wife and it is my duty to protect her. I decide who is permitted in her presence and who is not. Not you. Me." It was Darcy's turn to sneer, and years of pent up anger poured out of him, visible in his countenance and audible in his words. "You arranged this marriage. You insisted on it, even when she was unwilling. Now you will deal with me behaving as a husband and a gentleman should in regards to her." His point made, he stepped back. "We have a ball to attend. Wickham is not invited. I expect him gone before we return." He extended his elbow to Elizabeth and, once she had tucked her hand beneath it, turned them both and walked down the hall and out the door.

The couple walked across the square to Matlock House. Their arrival, unexpectedly early and on foot, sporting injuries, caused a great deal of alarm for the residents.

"What happened?" Lady Matlock's cry of alarm as she stood in the doorway of the drawing room brought her husband and sons running to her side.

"Good heavens!" Lord Matlock stepped around his wife and urged Darcy and Elizabeth into the room. He dismissed the butler, who had let the couple in, then shut the doors behind them.

Lady Matlock escorted Elizabeth to a settee and made her sit down. "Tansley, ring the bell. This arm will require ice or something. Her gloves will cover part of the mark, but not all. Elizabeth, tell us what happened. Darcy, come sit beside her. Are you injured, as well?"

Darcy lifted his right hand and examined it. Flexing the fingers, he winced. "Just this."

Lady Matlock shook her head and tsked at him. "What in the world happened today?"

Darcy gritted his teeth. "George Wickham accosted Elizabeth."

"What?" Tansley's shocked question was overridden by his brother's shouted, "That bounder!"

Lady Matlock immediately looked into Elizabeth's eyes. "Are you well?" Her soft question had a ring of steel to it.

Elizabeth nodded. "I am. He tried to kiss me and twisted my arm behind my back when I objected."

"And that is when Darcy's fist became bruised?" The countess' fierce look returned to her nephew's hand.

"Yes." Elizabeth kept her reply brief, because a maid entered with a bowl of ice and a towel.

"Bring those to me, Molly, and then you may leave." Lady Matlock's command was instantly followed and within moments, the door was closing again.

"What else happened?" Lord Matlock's question brought all eyes from Elizabeth to him.

Darcy explained the remainder of the events as best he could, with input from Elizabeth. He finished with a sigh. "I lost my temper. That has never happened before. I saw Wickham with his hands on my wife and I just ..." He shrugged. "I lost control."

"How did your father react?" Richard stood nearly at attention, his face like stone.

Darcy shrugged again. "I do not know. Once I said my piece, I dragged Elizabeth over here without waiting for him or a carriage." He reached for Elizabeth's hand, picking it up and kissing it. "I am sorry, love."

Elizabeth smiled softly. "All is well. I was eager to leave, and there is no better way to expel extreme emotion than to exercise."

Darcy smiled briefly at her, then his attention was caught by his family.

"I am going over there," Lord Matlock announced. "I suspect he will refuse to attend tonight, but I am not having it."

"I am going with you." The colonel moved to stand beside his father.

"I am, as well. Perhaps once he sees the full force of the Fitzwilliam family in opposition to him, he will behave. At least for this one night." Tansley joined his father and brother.

"I want you to know how proud of you I am, Darcy. I know you lost your temper, but I think it was needed. You put Elizabeth's needs ahead of yours. That is what a gentleman does." Matlock stared fiercely at his nephew as though willing him to understand. "And, I apologize again for believing his tales and not defending you all these years."

"Thank you, Uncle. I confess, it felt good to stand up to him. Should I go with you?"

"No, you stay here. Guests may begin to trickle in before we get back."

Darcy nodded his acceptance of his uncle's decision, and he and Elizabeth and their aunt watched the earl and his sons leave the room.

An hour later, the three of them had just stepped into the entry hall to form the reception line when the gentlemen returned, with George in tow. Lord Matlock exchanged a look with his wife as he took his place beside her, his lips in a firm, straight line. Tansley and the colonel silently slid into place beside their mother. George took a spot beside Richard. He lifted his nose in the air and, though he completely ignored his son and daughter, anger poured off him in waves.

Darcy and Elizabeth spent the remainder of the evening in a state of nervous anticipation. They had no idea what the earl had said to George, but they were fully cognizant of the fact that the older man was angry and would no doubt take it out on them. They endeavored to ignore him as much as possible, though Elizabeth was required to stand up with him for a set. Thankfully, he asked for the second set and Lady Matlock called a jig and another fast-moving dance, so conversation was nearly impossible.

At the end of the night, Lady Matlock declared the event a success. Elizabeth had been introduced to more people than she could possibly remember, and while not everyone welcomed her warmly, few treated her poorly.

<center>~~~***~~~</center>

To the young couple's surprise, George did not abuse them any more harshly than normal the next day, despite the air rage that surrounded him. Wickham had disappeared, to Elizabeth's immense relief. She and Darcy discussed it in the library once his father had vanished for the day.

"It is as though we do not exist." She shook her head. "I do not object, but it is so strange. Did you ask your uncle about it?"

"He would not tell me what he said to Father." Darcy lifted a shoulder and dropped it. "He insisted it was taken care of and I was not to worry. I am not certain I like it, but I am too much relieved that we are being left alone to care."

"True." Elizabeth paused. "I was unable to speak privately to your aunt last night. Perhaps I can tomorrow, before the dinner party." She startled. "Do you suppose your father wishes the dinner to be cancelled?"

"Hmmm, I do not know. He has not said anything. I cannot imagine him forgetting about it, so I say we should assume he does not wish to cancel. After all, to do so at this late date will be a mark against him in society." Darcy rolled his eyes.

"Very true," Elizabeth agreed with a wry twist of her lips.

"How are the preparations coming?" Darcy had been sitting with his arm around her shoulders. He squeezed them now and kissed her hair.

"Very well. Lady Matlock instructed me in every detail and has been an immense help. She came over here a few days ago and spoke to Mrs. Bishop and Cook after they became uncooperative." As she spoke, Elizabeth toyed with a piece of ribbon she had used to mark her place in her book.

Darcy's lips turned down. "When my father passes, I intend to dismiss any servants who have been disobedient or disrespectful to either of us. It is ridiculous for a housekeeper and a cook to behave so to the mistress of a household. It will not be forgotten."

"Thank you for defending me again." Elizabeth smiled and poked Darcy in the side. "Promise me you will not become unforgiving and bitter. I should hate for you to turn into your father."

"Hey, now." Darcy twisted away from his wife's stiff, pointy finger. "I promise I will not turn into Father. You must make me a vow, though."

"You mean a vow other than to love and honor you?" Elizabeth's brow arched.

"You forgot obey, but yes, in addition to those." Darcy grabbed her finger when Elizabeth went to poke him again. "That hurts, love. You do not know your own power." He rubbed his side.

Elizabeth laughed. "I am sorry. I will stop." She reached between them and tried to rub his side. "What promise do you wish me to make?"

"Promise me you will tell me if I begin to become intolerable." Darcy became solemn as he spoke.

Elizabeth reached up and stroked his side whiskers. "I promise. I doubt you could be that way, but I vow to tell you, should you begin to be so."

"Thank you, love." Darcy kissed Elizabeth, brushing his lips tenderly over hers. Then, the pair of them snuggled into the sofa and spent the rest of the evening reading to each other.

Chapter 21

The next day, Darcy and Elizabeth were up earlier than usual. Elizabeth was a bundle of nerves. She had never hosted a dinner before, and though Lady Matlock had led her through every step of the exercise, she still worried that she had forgotten something and would embarrass herself and Darcy. The anxiety had caused her already-delicate stomach to revolt twice in the hour since she had risen.

"It will be well, my love." Darcy held her hand as he assured her of her fitness to be hostess to a society soiree. "My aunt will be here to handle anything you feel incapable of."

Elizabeth snorted. "That is just the problem. I fear I am incapable of any of it."

"Nonsense." Darcy spoke firmly. "You are just as capable as anyone. You have no one you need to impress. As much as I loathe my father's arrogance and conceit, he is correct to be proud of the Darcy name. You, my love, are very much a Darcy. I am already impressed with you, as are my aunt, uncle, and cousins. The only person you need to impress is yourself."

Elizabeth tilted her head, her nerves temporarily forgotten as she listened. "Not your father?"

Darcy snorted. "There is no need to impress him. He cares not if you and I succeed or fail and he never will."

A slow smile lifted Elizabeth's lips. "That is good to hear. I will push him and his approval, or lack thereof, out of my mind and simply do the best I can." She leaned over the corner of the table that separated her from Darcy and kissed him.

That evening, as Elizabeth greeted her guests, she felt her courage rise. She recognized many of the couples from her ball, and was happy to be able to accurately match faces to names. She watched Darcy from time to time, pleased to see his enjoyment of what he usually disliked … greeting guests. As a result of her observation, she was able to see his face light up when his friend walked into the house, followed by an older couple.

"Bingley. I am so pleased you could make it." Darcy returned his friend's bow and then shook the other gentleman's hand. He turned to his father, who had barely greeted the new arrivals. "Father, you remember Charles Bingley, do you not?"

"Indeed." The elder Darcy bowed shallowly to Bingley, his face a hard mask.

Darcy flashed a look at George but turned back to his friend, who looked at him with sympathy.

"You remember my parents, do you not?" Bingley gestured to the couple standing beside him.

"I do." Darcy bowed to his friend's parents. "Welcome to Darcy House. Please allow me to introduce my wife to you." He quickly completed the task and then watched with a pleased smile as Elizabeth charmed them. Once the trio had moved down the receiving line, he began to greet the other guests.

Eventually, the flood of people slowed to a trickle and then stopped. Lord Matlock excused himself for a moment, and the countess and Elizabeth headed toward the drawing room. Darcy made to follow them when George suddenly grabbed his arm and pulled him back. When Darcy turned toward his father, the older man grabbed him by his cravat and pulled him forward until they were nose-to-nose.

"Watch yourself tonight, Boy. I do not know why Matlock is suddenly taking such an interest in you, but I do not like being told what I will and will not do in my own home. You are still a minor and under my supervision and I'm telling you, if you put a toe out of line tonight, it will go hard on you. That precious sister of yours could be firmly out of reach if you are not careful. Do you understand me?"

Darcy stood stiffly listening to his father's threats, his jaw and fists clenched. He swallowed, as much to force his teeth apart as to moisten his tongue. "Yes, sir."

"Keep that high-in-the-instep chit I married you to in line, as well." George shook his son and then let him go.

At that moment, Lord Matlock appeared. "Are you coming to the drawing room?" He looked at his nephew, taking note of the young man's reddened countenance and rigid stance, then at his brother-in-law. "What has happened?"

"None of your business, my lord." George sneered at the earl before turning and marching toward the drawing room.

Lord Matlock's eyes narrowed as he watched the other man walk away. When Darcy stepped up beside him, the earl swung his head the other direction, his sharp eyes taking note of the crumpled state of his nephew's cravat and the young man's stiff demeanor. "Darcy?"

"It is nothing, Uncle. I was warned to be on my best behavior." Darcy shrugged. "It could have been much worse." He paused. "He is resentful that you took up for me."

Matlock nodded absently, his gaze straying back down the hall toward the drawing room. "I suspected that was so. I would be, as well, in his position." He turned back to Darcy. "Your cousins and I will protect you as best we are able tonight. If he becomes violent after we leave, send Elizabeth over to get us, or a servant, if necessary. Your man or her maid would be best."

"I will. I promise. Thank you." Darcy heaved a sigh. "I suppose we should go in."

Matlock clapped him on the shoulder. "Yes; we are expected."

Together, the gentlemen strode to the gathering, joining their wives and the rest of the party just as the gong sounded to announce the meal.

Because the dinner was a formal affair, diners were expected to go from the drawing room to the table according to precedence. There were four and twenty people in attendance, and since the dining room was just a little too small to fit everyone, the table had been carried to the ballroom and extra leaves added to it. As the guests entered, Elizabeth and her new aunt encouraged them to sit where ever they wished. As mistress of the house, Elizabeth was at one end of the table, with Darcy at her right hand. Lady Matlock sat to her left.

George, as master, sat at the other end. Lord Matlock sat to his left and Lady Cavendish to his right. Colonel Fitzwilliam seated himself nearer to his uncle's end of the table than to his cousin's, with the viscount following suit on the other side, so as to keep a closer eye on the elder Darcy.

It seemed that everyone at the table noticed George's foul mood. Few addressed him directly, and those who did received curt, harsh responses.

Darcy was pleased that his friend was close enough to engage him in a bit of conversation. He divided his attention between Bingley and Elizabeth, who he felt needed his calming touch now and then. He purposely ignored his father, knowing the other man could not hear his conversation and could have nothing disparaging to say about his manners or Elizabeth's.

The dinner proceeded through four courses with no mishaps. George drank perhaps more than he ate, but largely remained silent. His narrowed gaze often settled on his son and daughter-in-law.

Finally, the meal was over and it was time for the ladies to separate from the gentlemen.

Elizabeth rose, followed by Lady Matlock and the others. She led them across the hall to the drawing room.

"You are doing very well, Elizabeth." Lady Matlock's whispered encouragement made her niece's shoulders relax just a little.

"Thank you." Elizabeth hesitated. "William's father is angry. I could not hear what he said, but I noticed that he began to be left out of the conversation on that end."

"He is behaving as a buffoon." Lady Matlock sniffed. "So worried about his reputation, yet he allows himself to be directed by anger." She rolled her eyes and shook her head. "Do not worry about him. Matlock and the boys have been observing him closely. They will step in if necessary."

Elizabeth tipped her head. "I will try." She gave her aunt a small smile. "Thank you."

"You are welcome." The countess patted her arm. "Come now; let us mingle with the guests."

So it was that when the gentlemen finally appeared a quarter hour later, Elizabeth was deep in conversation with Lady Allen's daughters, Lady Penelope and Lady Helen, and Lord and Lady Walker's daughter, Lady Hannah. She smiled at Darcy when he came up behind her and touched her shoulder, but was too absorbed in the discussion to do more.

Darcy was pleased to see his wife making friends, as he supposed she was. He did not wish for her to become too isolated, as he often had been, before he went to University. He looked around for Bingley, who along with Richard, had been his closest friend for the past four years.

Just then, his friend approached, a drink in his hand and a smile on his face. "Excellent party, Darcy. You should be proud of your wife."

"Oh, I am. She has done very well, and I know my aunt is pleased with her." Darcy gestured to a pair of chairs at the side of the room. He and his friend seated themselves and began catching up on their news.

Soon, the single ladies took turns at the pianoforte, providing music for the company. The rest of the guests were sprinkled around the room in small groups. Some paid close attention to the performances, while others maintained quiet conversations.

Elizabeth, who was keeping a close eye on all the guests so she could make sure they were enjoying themselves, noticed George Darcy sitting in the back of the room near a group of other gentlemen, but not so close as to be considered part of it. She saw him scowl, and her brow creased as she wondered what had caused it. Looking around, she saw her husband and his friend deep in conversation and wondered if that was the cause of George's glare.

After the ladies had all exhibited and several rounds of cards were played, it was time for the guests to leave. Elizabeth and Darcy made their farewells to everyone, including the Matlock party, and turned to go upstairs and retire. They were exhausted and hoped to avoid George's notice. Their hope was in vain.

"Get in here!" The elder Darcy's voice roared at them from the drawing room doorway.

"Father, it is late and we are exhausted. Can we discuss it on the morrow?" Darcy stiffened his spine. He did not wish to have a confrontation at all, but if he must, he would rather do it when he was not so tired.

"I said get in here." George stalked into the hallway, fists clenched. "When I tell you to do something, you do it." He drew back a hand as though to strike one of them.

Without a word, Darcy turned toward the drawing room. He gestured for Elizabeth to go upstairs, but his father forestalled that.

"Her, too."

Lips pressed together, Darcy strode into the drawing room, Elizabeth at his side.

"You pay that tradesman's son far too much attention. I do not know what the countess was thinking to allow you to invite him. You will break off that connection immediately. I will not have my name associated with persons of such low standing."

Darcy's jaw dropped. "Low standing? Bingley and his family are accepted into the highest circles. Welcomed, even!"

"I do not care if Prinny himself has taken a liking to the upstart. You will not associate with him."

Darcy crossed his arms. "I will not give him up."

Elizabeth tucked her hand under her husband's elbow as she addressed her father-in-law. "You are closely associated with the son of your steward, which is no better than a tradesman. You do not have room to talk. William will not give Mr. Bingley's friendship up." She lifted her chin in defiance.

"You will do as I say or you will be out on the streets!"

Darcy lifted his chin, as well. "We will pack our bags immediately." He lowered his arms.

Enraged, George stepped close and swung his fist at his son's head. Darcy leaped backwards, jerking Elizabeth back with him.

This successful evasion of his attack only served to anger George further. He charged at the young couple, arms outstretched. Elizabeth had let go of her husband's arm as they scrambled backwards, and when the older man rushed forward and began swinging his fists, she was caught in the shoulder and thrown to the floor, landing on a footstool and breaking it.

For Darcy, seeing his wife fall at the hand of his father was a nightmare come true. He could not go to her aid, despite that being his greatest desire, because he was occupied with warding off George's blows. When Elizabeth did not instantly arise, instead remaining still, fear of losing her or the child they were both certain she was carrying chilled his blood, followed closely by an anger fiercer than anything else he had ever known. With his uncle's words ringing in his ears and a red haze clouding his vision as it had done before, Darcy began to fight back, grateful for the lessons in pugilism his cousin had insisted he receive at University.

Though the men were equally matched in size, George had his age and years of dissolute behavior to slow him down. Darcy, on the other hand, was quick and light of foot. The two traded blows for several minutes. George was starting to falter when the door burst open and footmen began to rush in, tearing them apart. Darcy was dragged backwards, away from his father. He fought to free himself.

"Easy now, sir. That will be enough." The servant holding his right arm adjusted his grip, moving slightly in front of Darcy's body.

After a few moments, the haze over his vision began to clear and Darcy stopped struggling as hard. Then, he saw his wife, who had propped herself up on her side. "Elizabeth!" He began to struggle harder. "Let me go. She needs me!"

"Throw him out! Throw them both out! Do it now!" George shouted instructions to the servants, who froze momentarily but then moved to obey.

Suddenly, a deep voice from the doorway stopped them. "Let him go. Mr. and Mrs. Darcy will be going nowhere for now." The authority in the words made the men jump to obey. When George protested, he was reminded that an earl outranked a mere gentleman.

George inhaled, puffing up so far that he was in danger of popping his buttons, his countenance turning an even deeper shade of red as he sputtered. "This is my house and I say who stays or goes!"

Ignoring the other gentleman's words, Lord Matlock stalked into the room, Viscount Tansley and the colonel behind him. He strode across the chamber to stand in front of his late sister's fuming husband. "I warned you a mere two nights ago what would happen if harm befell my nephew and his wife. Did I not? And yet, here I stand, in your house, to break up fisticuffs between you and your only son." The earl shook his head. When George tried to speak, the earl raised his voice. "Darcy and Elizabeth will not be leaving this house. You will. At first light. You will go to Pemberley and you will remain there. The countess and I will follow, and we will be taking Georgiana with us." Matlock shook his finger in George's florid, scowling face. "She had best be in pristine condition when we arrive."

George's jaw jutted out. "What if I refuse?"

"In that case, I will appeal to the courts for custody. There is a plethora of evidence to show that you have no business raising children. Would that I had seen it years ago. I will live the rest of my life with regret for failing my sister's only son." Matlock shook his head. "I will separate the house of Matlock from the house of Darcy, and I will not be shy to explain to all I know the reasons for such a breach. You have two choices, Brother. You can retire to Pemberley and maintain your social status and acceptance, or you can remain in London and be ruined. The decision is yours." Lord Matlock waited while George protested, cursing him out and punching walls. When George's rage and bluster diminished and he acquiesced, the earl followed Darcy, Elizabeth, and their servants up the stairs, making certain as he went that the physician had been summoned.

The viscount and his brother watched their father disappear from the doorway, then turned as one to their uncle.

"Father has had his turn with you; now it is ours." Richard took a step closer to George, leaning in until his nose and his uncle's were a hair's breadth apart. "You have spent years abusing a defenseless child. I am proud of my cousin for finally standing up to you."

Tansley nodded in the background. "I am, as well."

Richard lifted his lips in a half smile. "I can see you are angry. Enraged, even." He chuckled when George's eyes flickered over his shoulder and his jaw clenched. "Tell you what. I will let you take that out on me. Let us see if you can take abuse as well as you give it."

The three were silent as George Darcy stared into his youngest nephew's eyes. For several ticks of the clock, they were deadlocked, with no one moving, even to blink. Finally, with a huff, George pushed past Richard and Tansley.

"He is a coward at heart, just like I always suspected." Richard laughed, nudging his brother with an elbow.

"Typical of a bully." Tansley slapped the colonel on the shoulder. "Good work. We should go up and see what else is happening. Mother will want a full report."

"After you." Richard gave a half-bow, extending his arm in invitation to his brother.

Chapter 22

On the third floor, Elizabeth was with her maid in the dressing room, preparing to see the doctor when he arrived. Darcy was sitting in a chair in front of the cold fireplace, his uncle standing beside him with his hand on the younger man's shoulder.

Richard and his brother stepped into the room through the open door. "What are you doing way up here? Why are your rooms not downstairs?"

Darcy looked wearily up at his cousins before glancing around the room. "My father assigned us this room when we came back from our wedding trip." He shrugged. "To be honest, we prefer it at this point. It is far enough away from him that we are left alone."

Tansley settled into the chair next to Darcy's. "I can certainly understand that."

"Yes," Richard said. "I would feel the same."

Lord Matlock said nothing, merely pulling the corners of his lips down.

Tansley tipped his head toward the dressing room. "How is Elizabeth?"

Darcy's brow wrinkled as his gaze flitted to the dressing room door and back. "She says she is well, but I insist she allow the physician to attend her. We -" He looked down at the floor. "We suspect her to be with child." He dropped his head in his hands, elbows on his knees.

Lord Matlock pressed his lips tighter together as he squeezed his nephew's shoulder.

Richard growled. "If I had known that ten minutes ago …" He let the thought dangle.

"I am happy you did not. While I would very much like a piece of my uncle, I would not wish him dead, and you surely would have killed him." Tansley gave his brother a pointed look.

At that moment, Elizabeth came out of the dressing room, walking slowly and supported by her maid. She was swathed from her neck to her toes in her tightly-buttoned dressing gown and slippers, but seeing all the gentlemen made her blush.

The earl and his sons turned red, as well, but they were too concerned with her to leave right away. Darcy lurched to his feet, wincing at the movement, and came to her side. "Are you well?"

Elizabeth looked up at her husband's bruised and battered face. She lifted a hand to gently stroke his side whiskers. "I am, so far. I am sore and there are bruises, but I will be well, no matter what happens."

Darcy stared deep into her eyes. He lifted her hand and kissed it, then leaned down to kiss her lips. "I love you," he whispered.

"I love you, too." Elizabeth glanced behind her husband to see Smith lingering in the doorway. "Your valet requires your attention."

Darcy nodded. "Let me help you into bed."

Elizabeth glanced at the earl and his sons and blushed darker, but agreed. She kept her dressing gown on and climbed into the bed. Darcy pulled the covers up to her chin, kissing her softly and doing his best to hide his grimace of pain. Straightening, he turned and entered the adjoining room, followed by his relatives.

As Smith helped him out of his tailcoat and cravat, Darcy turned his focus on his uncle. "How did you know to come over here? I did not have time to send for you."

Lord Matlock took a seat in Darcy's shaving chair. "A footman ran over and told my butler that help was required. The butler came upstairs and got me."

"We …" Richard motioned between himself and the viscount. "… were playing billiards and heard the knock on the door. We were waiting for Father when he came down the stairs."

"I am certain the neighbors were shocked to see our mad dash across the square." Tansley chuckled.

The gentlemen continued discussing the night's events while Smith attended to Darcy's swollen and bloody knuckles and bruised face and torso. The physician arrived in the midst of this, and looked in on Darcy before he began his examination of Elizabeth.

"Have you any other injuries?" The doctor, a Mr. Westcott, lifted his patient's hands one at a time, bending the fingers at each joint.

"There are some bruises on my chest." Darcy winced when Mr. Westcott poked at his newly-blackened eye.

"How is the pain? Do you feel any movement in the ribs?"

"The pain is not excessive, and no, I do not feel movement."

"Take your shirt off, Darcy, and let him see. There is no point in diminishing your injuries." Lord Matlock drilled his nephew with his insistent gaze.

With a sigh, Darcy obeyed.

The physician poked and prodded some more, laying his ear against his patient's chest. Finally, he stood. "I can feel nothing broken, nor can I hear bones grating together. I concur with your evaluation, Mr. Darcy, that you are merely bruised. It is nothing to take lightly, of course. I see your man has some ice chunks in that bowl; they should be applied for a quarter hour or so at a time to reduce the swelling. I can administer a pain reliever, if you desire one."

Darcy shook his head. "No, thank you. Smith has laid in a supply of willow bark recently. That will suffice. I need no opiates. Of greater concern to me is my wife."

Westcott smiled. "It was she who insisted that you be attended to first. There is nothing better than a devoted wife."

Darcy ducked his head and lifted his lips in a small smile. "I agree." He looked at Westcott again. "I expect a report from you after the examination."

"Of course. I will return shortly."

As it turned out, Smith was finished with Darcy before the doctor completed Elizabeth's examination. Darcy thanked his uncle and cousins for their assistance, asked his valet to see them out, and slipped into the bed chamber.

Dr. Westcott was sitting in a chair at the side of the bed, writing something in a journal. He did not move when Darcy seated himself on the bed at Elizabeth's side. Instead, he steadily wrote until he was finished, at which time he stood, bowed again to Darcy, and sat back down.

"How is she?" Darcy took Elizabeth's hand but looked expectantly at the doctor.

"I am fine, William." Elizabeth squeezed her husband's hand.

Darcy glanced at his wife and raised her fingers to kiss them, but continued to stare at Westcott.

"Mrs. Darcy is much as you are: bruised. She has no broken bones, though her left arm has suffered a sprain. She is to keep it as immobile as possible for the next week or so. I will come back in seven to ten days to check on her." Westcott paused. "As for the child, she has not miscarried as of this moment. That does not mean it will not happen. Nor does it mean it will." He shrugged. "There is much we do not know about pregnancy. I am not one who subscribes to the idea that women are helpless, useless creatures or that miscarriage is the fault of the mother. I have explained the signs to your wife and informed her that I am to be summoned immediately, should she experience any of them."

Darcy nodded solemnly. "Very good."

Westcott stood, tucking his ledger into the inside pocket of his coat. "I have described to the maid a contraption made of cloth that will keep that arm in place. If you fail to use it, you could cause yourself irreparable damage."

"I understand. I will use it." Elizabeth looked the doctor in the eye. "Thank you, sir."

"Yes, thank you." Darcy rose. "I will walk you to the door."

Westcott waved him away. "I know my way out. You stay here and rest." He bowed again and stepped into the hall, closing the door behind him.

Darcy turned back to the bed and pulled down the covers on his side. He started to remove his dressing gown. "I am ready to go to sleep. Is there anything I can get for you before we blow out the candles?"

"I must use the chamber pot, but other than that, no. I am exhausted and eager for bed, as well."

"I will help you up. Do not move." Darcy hastened around the end of the bed, then drew back the covers and helped Elizabeth up. He escorted her into the dressing room, his arm around her waist, and when she was finished, helped her back into the bed. Then, he retraced his path to his side and climbed in. He pulled her close, taking care that he did not touch her arm or any bruises, and laid his head on the pillow next to hers. Within moments, both were asleep.

~~~***~~~

The next day, Darcy and Elizabeth slept late. When they finally awakened, they groaned in unison, as their bodies had stiffened up during the night and their various bumps and bruises were making their presence known.

"Shall we remain in our rooms today, do you think?" Darcy had tried to get up but in the end, laid back down and snuggled up to his wife.

"I would like it if we could." Elizabeth lifted her hand and stroked her husband's cheek. "Dare we try?"

"I say yes, we do dare. If my father has not left for Pemberley as my uncle told him to, we will deal with it. Hopefully, he is long gone." Darcy kissed Elizabeth's forehead and then her lips, then rested his head on her pillow. Soon, they were both asleep again.

A short while later, they were brought out of their nap by the sound of a clearing throat.

"Mr. Darcy?" Smith pitched his voice low. If Darcy was not too deeply asleep, he would hear. Otherwise, the valet knew to try again later.

Darcy jumped a little and then yawned.

"Mr. Darcy?" Smith spoke a little louder this time.
~~~

"Yes?" Darcy croaked. He cleared his throat and repeated himself, looking up at the servant who approached the foot of the bed.

Smith kept his eyes averted as he spoke. "Lord and Lady Matlock were here a short while ago. When I told them you were still sleeping, they said they would return in a few hours, before they left for their evening entertainment."

Darcy nodded. "My father?"

"Mr. George Darcy left for Pemberley at dawn on horseback. Carstairs followed in one of the carriages an hour or so later."

Darcy breathed a sigh of relief. "Thank goodness. I did not relish facing him this morning." He paused. "Not that it will be any better in a month after he has had time to fume about it."

"No, sir." Smith pressed his lips tightly together for a moment. "Shall I have bathwater brought up?"

Darcy looked down at Elizabeth, who had awakened during his conversation but remained silent. When she nodded, he moved his gaze back to his employee. "Yes, please. And bring that deep tub back in here. Father will not need it and it is better for soaking in than the shallow one we have been using. Oh, and have something brought up so we can break our fasts."

With a bow and an "As you wish," Smith turned around and left Darcy and Elizabeth to themselves.

~~~***~~~

Five days later, Darcy and Elizabeth were sitting in the drawing room, reading to each other, when the doorbell rang. They looked up, but hearing Mr. Baxter answer the summons, went back to their occupation. They were surprised when the butler knocked on the door and requested permission to enter the room.

Darcy sat up from his slouched position on the sofa and waved the servant into the room. His brows shot up to see the missive in Mr. Baxter's hand.

"An express rider brought this. I sent him around to the kitchens for something to eat. I do not know if a reply is required." The butler extended the paper to Darcy, who accepted it.

"I will send word." Darcy dismissed the servant.

"Who is it from?" Elizabeth had straightened from her position tucked into her husband's side. She now peeked over his shoulder.

Darcy's brow creased as he examined the direction. "I am uncertain." He turned the letter over and broke the seal. Unfolding it, he glanced
~~~

first at the bottom. "This is from Carstairs! Why would he be writing to me?" Swiftly, he read through the note, his eyes widening. When he finished, he read it again. His heart pounded and his mouth went dry. Upon completing his second perusal, he lowered the hand holding the letter to his lap and stared unseeingly across the room.

"William? What does it say?" When Darcy did not reply, Elizabeth took the missive from his hand and began to read it herself. "Oh!" She read further. "Oh, my!" She dropped the note in her lap and lifted her hand to caress his side whiskers. "How do you feel, my love? I do not know what to say."

Darcy shook his head. "I do not know how I feel." He reached up and grasped Elizabeth's fingers in his own, kissing them and holding them to his chest. "I …" He sighed. "Numb, perhaps? I cannot help but wonder if it is real; if he is really dead or if this is some sort of cruel deception that will lead to some other abuse."

Elizabeth nodded sadly. "Perhaps we should ask Uncle Henry for assistance?"

"Yes, I think you are right." Darcy took a deep breath and let it out slowly. "Do you think I should be crying, if it is true?"

"I do not know." Elizabeth looked down. "I confess that I am joyful inside at the thought of being free of him. I feel terribly guilty about it, but those are my feelings."

"Yes." Darcy bit his lip. "I feel the same, I think." He shook his head. "I do not know. I should not say that, I suppose. I cannot make any sense of the emotions roiling around inside me at the moment." He kissed her fingers again, then rose to his feet and walked to the fireplace. There, he rang the bell.

When Baxter appeared once more, Darcy instructed him to send someone across to Matlock House and summon the earl and countess.

"What about the messenger?" The butler tilted his head as he waited for instructions.

Darcy licked his lips. "If he can wait a little longer, it would be best. I have no reply at present but might after I speak to my uncle. If waiting is not possible, pay him and dismiss him and I will hire someone later."

"Very good, sir." Baxter bowed and left the room.

Less than a quarter hour later, Lord and Lady Matlock stepped into the drawing room. Without a word, Darcy handed the earl the express he had received.

Lord Matlock immediately read the missive. "Oh, my." He paused and swallowed. "I do not know what to say."

"What, Henry? What has happened?" Lady Matlock reached for the letter, but her arms were not long enough to retrieve it from her husband, who was reading the words again.

"If this is correct, our brother is dead."

"What?" Lady Matlock's hand went to her throat. "How?"

The earl shook his head. "It does not say." He peered at the closing. "Carstairs?"

Darcy nodded. "Father's valet." He paused. "Could it be real? I mean …" He stood and began to pace. "How do we know it is not a test of some sort and that he will not try to abuse me in some manner upon my arrival at Pemberley?"

Lady Matlock gasped, but her husband understood Darcy better. "Anything is possible, but judging by the unsteadiness of the penmanship in this missive, it truly happened." He stood up. "In case it is true, we need to contact George's solicitor. You should prepare to leave for Pemberley. I will go home and write the letters for you and make the arrangements. You may take one of our carriages if you do not have one here."

"I will go with them." Lady Matlock made her declaration as she stood to her feet. "If it is true, they will need assistance. Neither of them has had to handle something like this before. If it is not true, they may be in need of protection. I am not able to physically do so, but my presence alone should keep George calm enough."

"That is a sound idea. I will follow as soon as I can." The earl stepped up to his nephew and placed a hand on his shoulder. Squeezing lightly, he said, "You are not alone, Darcy. We will never again leave you to the mercy of someone or something else."

Emotion filled Darcy's throat, choking him. "Thank you," he whispered.

Chapter 23

Early the following morning, Darcy joined his wife and aunt in the Darcy travelling coach. He tapped on the roof with his walking stick and the equipage lurched into motion.

"Your uncle has instructed the coachman to travel as expeditiously as possible. The note you received indicated your father was packed in ice, but it is July and ice melts quickly. By the time we arrive, he will have been dead a week. You will have to have him buried as soon as possible."

Darcy swallowed. "Yes." He closed his eyes for a moment, squeezing Elizabeth's hand, which he had grasped in his as soon as he entered the vehicle. "It is all so strange." He shook his head. "I am still uncertain if I should believe it."

"We will find out soon enough," Elizabeth whispered. "Let us hope for the best, whatever that might be."

Darcy nodded and with that, the three fell silent for a short time. It was the countess who broke the silence after they had stopped to change horses.

"Elizabeth, did you not say your family is in Hertfordshire?"

"I did." Elizabeth turned her gaze from the window to Lady Matlock. "They are near Meryton, but we will not have time to stop. The village is too far off the main road."

"No, I know. I am sorry for that." The countess paused. "You never visited your family in London, either, did you?"

Elizabeth shrugged. "There really was not time, and after the confrontation at breakfast that day, I was not prepared to request permission."

Darcy had watched his wife carefully as she spoke. "How do you feel about that now? I recall that you were not very much concerned about it before."

"I am still unconcerned, to be honest. I would like an explanation, an apology, even, but it can wait." Elizabeth sighed and looked at her hands, currently clasped in her lap. "I am making the choice to forgive, not only my uncle and aunt but my parents. I find I must do it again every day."

"Have you heard from any of them?" Lady Matlock tilted her head as she examined her niece, trying to determine how the girl really felt.

"I have exchanged letters with my eldest sister several times, and with my younger sister once or twice. The two youngest added sentiments to Mary's letter but have not written me directly. I have heard nothing from my parents. I suppose Mama is pleased I am married and she will be saved from the hedgerows when Papa passes." Elizabeth pressed her lips together and looked out the window.

Darcy reached over and took one of his wife's hands. He lifted it to his lips, pressed a kiss to the back, and intertwined his fingers with hers before resting them together on his thigh.

Elizabeth smiled softly at Darcy. "I am grateful and blessed to have been given to William. Everything could have been so much worse." She turned back to Lady Matlock. "That makes it easier to forgive my parents, to be honest."

"Good." Lady Matlock smiled. "You two make a handsome couple, and I knew right away that you had fallen in love. I find it a wonder that my brother-in-law never noticed it."

Darcy explained the situation. "We endeavored to hide our affection as much as we could. I knew he might try to separate us if he realized how we felt, so we remained as formal as possible when in company." His brow creased slightly as he tipped his head to stare at his aunt. "How is it you knew?"

The countess chuckled. "It was as clear as day whenever your eyes met. I have not seen such adoration on another's face in a long time."

Darcy and Elizabeth exchanged wide-eyed glances, but then laughed.

"Perhaps the next trip, we might stop and speak to your family?" Darcy rubbed his thumb over Elizabeth's hand as he spoke.

Elizabeth shrugged again. "Perhaps."

~~~***~~~

The journey to Derbyshire was a grueling one. They made the same number of stops as usual, but did not tarry. Instead, as soon as the horses where changed for a fresh set, they were back on the road. Many times, the occupants did not get out to even stretch their legs. They ate the first day out of a hamper packed by the cook at Matlock House. They spent one night on the road, finally arriving at the estate well after dark the second day.

Darcy had been watching, and as the carriage entered the gate, saw lit torches surrounding a large, black wreath that hung there. He gasped and gripped his wife's hand.

Elizabeth and Lady Matlock looked out Darcy's window and saw the wreath. They leaned back.

"So, it is true." Lady Matlock sighed. "Surely if it were a ruse, George would not go so far as to hang mourning about the place."
~~~

"No, that would be a bit extreme, even for him." Darcy swallowed down the feelings rising within him.

A few minutes later, the carriage came to a stop in front of the courtyard. The housekeeper had placed several candelabras across the large span, lighting the space up as though it were daylight. Even from the drive, a mourning wreath on the door stood out to those exiting the coach. With a deep breath, Darcy escorted his wife and aunt to the other side and into the house.

"Welcome home, sir." Mrs. Reynolds curtseyed. "On behalf of the entire staff, I extend my condolences."

His mien blank and stiff, Darcy nodded. He cleared his throat. "Thank you. Has my father been prepared for burial?"

"Yes, sir. Carstairs performed the office as soon as he arrived at Pemberley with the master. We packed the body in fresh ice and have been refilling it every day. He hired someone to arrange everything else."

"Good." Darcy darted a glance at first Elizabeth and then Lady Matlock. "I wish to see him, and will need to speak to Carstairs, but as it is late, I suppose it can wait until morning. Have our rooms been prepared?"

"Yes, sir." Mrs. Reynolds gripped her hands together in front of her. "I did not know what you wished to do about your rooms, so I left you and Mrs. Darcy in the suite you resided in on your prior stay. Lady Matlock is in a suite in the family wing. The staff is waiting to bring up bathwater or whatever else may be needed."

Darcy looked at his aunt. "What can we have sent to you, Aunt Audra?"

"Some tea and cold meats and cheeses will do for now, and whatever sweets the cook may have on hand." Lady Matlock addressed the housekeeper. "I would like a bath, as well. Have our servants arrived?"

"Yes, ma'am, and I have also had your luggage carried up."

"Then that is all I require. I will have my maid make any further requests." The countess dismissed Mrs. Reynold with a brisk nod.

"Mrs. Darcy and I would like the same brought up to us. We will remain in the rooms we had before for the time being." Darcy turned as the housekeeper acknowledged his words and headed toward the stairs with Elizabeth on his arm and his aunt following.

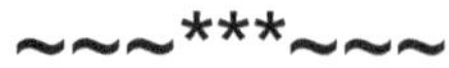

"Elizabeth, you and I will begin writing out the notifications today, unless we have visitors. If word of George's demise has spread to the local estates, the ladies could show up here to sit with us." Lady Matlock spoke as she stirred her tea at breakfast the following morning.

"Has the paper been purchased? I assume it has, given everything else that has been completed, but I have not seen it." Elizabeth lifted her eyes to her aunt as she took a sip of tea.

"We will ask Reynolds. If it has not, then of course, we must wait, but it should be done as soon as possible." The countess cast a critical eye over her niece. "Are you well? You look a bit pale."

Elizabeth sighed. "Something is not agreeing with me." Her brow creased as she used her fork to push the food around on her plate. "I suspect it is the child causing the issue." She laid a hand on her still-flat belly. "He does like to vex me at the most inopportune moments." She smirked.

Lady Matlock chuckled. "They all do, I think." She paused. "You are blessed to have not lost the babe. I have thanked the good Lord daily for His mercy."

Elizabeth smiled. "I have, as well." Her hand rubbed the spot where her baby rested. "I am eager to finally feel him move."

Lady Matlock opened her mouth to speak when Darcy entered the room. She closed it and watched as her nephew went straight to his wife's side to lean down and give her a soft kiss and a greeting. Her lips lifted in a tender smile. When Darcy had filled a plate and seated himself, she asked what he had learned.

"Father was killed in a brawl over a game of cards. Stabbed." Darcy rested his hands at the side of his plate and stared at the table. He took a breath, opened his mouth, and then closed it again. Finally, he spoke. "He was winning and one of the other players objected and suggested Father must be cheating. He was still enraged about what Carstairs termed my 'insolence' and challenged his accuser to prove his claim. They fought and the other man pulled a knife. Carstairs said he was stabbed at least a dozen times." He closed his eyes for a moment. When he opened them, his brow wrinkled and a tortured expression briefly crossed his features. "He blames me for Father's death." Speaking over the gasps of his tablemates, he continued. "He insisted that had I not been disobedient and rebellious, my father would still be live, because he would have had a cooler head and would have appeased his killer instead of aggravating him."

Elizabeth reached her hand out to rest over his. When Darcy turned his over and laced his fingers with hers, she squeezed. "Carstairs is wrong. You know this."

Darcy took a deep breath. He focused his gaze on his wife. "I do, but it still hurt to hear his words."

"That is what he wanted." Lady Matlock spoke crisply. "Your uncle will speak to him. He will be let go without a reference if I have my way."

No one replied to the countess' statement. Elizabeth urged Darcy to eat, only sitting back and relinquishing his hand when he complied.

"What time is the funeral?" Elizabeth waited to inquire until her husband had eaten a good portion of the food on his plate.

"Noon." Darcy glanced at the clock. "Mr. Wickham was here right before I came down to eat. He will direct the mourners to the formal parlor. He is certain at least a few of the neighbors will come."

"We are prepared either way." Elizabeth's quiet assurance made Darcy visibly relax. When he was done eating, he took her hand again and kissed it. She smiled at him, and then leaned over to whisper in his ear. "I love you. I am proud of you."

Darcy squeezed her hand with a smile and a matching whisper.

~~~***~~~

That evening, after the funeral was over and the mourners were gone home, Darcy and Elizabeth retired to their chambers. A newly dyed black gown hung in Elizabeth's closet, and Darcy had new black armbands for his coat, as well a black hatband. The couple reclined on the sofa in front of the open balcony doors, enjoying the breeze that gently blew over them. Darcy played with the edge of the sling that held Elizabeth's arm in position.

"You know you are master of Pemberley now, do you not?" Elizabeth watched his hand as his long fingers picked and pulled at the material.

Darcy's movement paused for a heartbeat and then began again. "It does not seem real. I expect him to call me to his study at any moment to berate me and mock me."

Elizabeth made a noise like a hum. "I agree. It seems strange." Craning her neck, she looked up at her husband. "How do you feel? Can you identify it yet?"

Darcy shrugged. "I have felt numb most of the day. I felt tears rising during the service but held them back." He sighed. "What I feel most is, I
~~~

think, regret. I wish he had been the father I needed." He shrugged again. "I do not know that I can explain it any better than that."

"I understand what you are saying, I think." Elizabeth paused for a moment. "I had my father's attention and affection all my life, until the day he informed me of my impending marriage. You never had that." She leaned her head against Darcy's shoulder. "I wish it had been better for you, as well. What you had to deal with was horrible."

"If it had not been for my sister, I would have run away long ago." Darcy rested his cheek on his wife's hair. "In my mind, she has always been part of my inheritance. If I lost Pemberley, I would lose the ability to protect her, to keep Father's attention off her and onto me."

"Do you regret it?"

"No!" Darcy shook his head, his whiskers messing up Elizabeth's hair. "I would do it again if it were required."

"She held up very well sitting with us during the funeral."

"She did the same when we told her of his passing. I expected more tears than she produced, but she really did not know him well. He rarely visited her, and I made sure to keep him directed elsewhere." Darcy kissed the top of his wife's head.

"Mmm." Elizabeth thought for several minutes. "I am glad we did not force her to remain in the nursery. I know women and children are thought too sensitive to endure death and all the ceremonies around it, but she needed us."

"She did." Darcy paused. "We must wait for Uncle Henry before we assume I am master. Father's will may not be written in my favor."

"I hope it is, for your sake." Elizabeth lifted her face for a kiss.

Chapter 24

Lord Matlock arrived at Pemberley the day after the funeral. After refreshing himself, he joined the countess and the Darcys in the family parlor, except for Georgiana, who had retired to the nursery for the evening.

"What have you learned?" Darcy implored his uncle for information the moment greetings were exchanged.

The earl settled into a seat on a settee beside his wife. He leaned back with a weary sigh. "I am your guardian until you reach one and twenty."

"My birthday is in a little over three weeks." Darcy reached for Elizabeth's hand.

The earl tipped his head in acknowledgement. "True. By the time the will goes through probate, you will have reached your majority."

"How will that affect his inheritance?" Lady Matlock changed her position slightly so as to be able to see her husband without craning her neck.

"I know no other manner of explaining it than to simply say it." Lord Matlock turned his eyes to Darcy, brows lifted. "Your inheritance will not be handed over to you until Elizabeth is found to be with child."

While the ladies gasped, Darcy nodded. "He said exactly that. Was there no mention of the sixth month of marriage?"

"There was. I am uncertain how the court will deal with such an unorthodox instruction. However, if my niece is, indeed, with child now, come the sixth month of your marriage, anyone looking at her will know."

Darcy kissed Elizabeth's hand. He looked back at the earl and bit his lip. "Were there any other requirements?"

Matlock shook his head. "Not from you. Apparently, he was unconcerned with a live birth."

"So, November comes and I am clearly going to have a baby, and the court grants William his inheritance … what does that entail? What about Georgiana? Will you retain guardianship, Uncle, or will William be given that? And, what of Mr. Wickham?" Elizabeth's questions burst forth, as though she had been holding them in for a long time and could not do so any longer.

Darcy had watched Elizabeth as she made her inquiries, and when she was finished, he turned again to his uncle. "Yes, what of Wickham?"

The earl rubbed his neck. "It will be as you told me your father indicated, should Elizabeth not retain this pregnancy. George Wickham will be handed the estate and you will receive nothing. If you do inherit everything, Wickham will receive an amount of money and the living at Kympton."

Darcy's eyes widened. His mouth fell open as he stared at his uncle. Finally, he closed it and swallowed. "You cannot be serious. George Wickham has no more business being a clergyman than my father did."

"Oh, but I am." The earl shrugged. "I agree with you wholeheartedly, but there it is."

"How much money?" Lady Matlock's eyes had narrowed at her husband's information.

"Ten thousand pounds."

"Ten thousand!" It was the countess' turn to be shocked. "That is a huge amount. What was he thinking?"

"That he preferred the steward's son over his own, most likely." Darcy's words were bitter.

"I am sorry, son." Lord Matlock gave Darcy a sympathetic look.

Elizabeth squeezed Darcy's hand. "It will all work out. We will be well."

"We have not seen the books as of yet, but I hope you are correct." Darcy gazed into his wife's eyes. "We may have to endure a few years of poverty before we are able to live as we ought. Will you mind?"

Elizabeth shook her head. She tipped it to indicate the large, elegant room. "I hardly think living in a house like this will be difficult. My father is a gentleman, but he is not as high as you, and our home was not as fine. We will manage. It will be well."

Darcy kissed her hand again. "Thank you." He turned to his uncle once more. "What of my sister?"

"She will remain under my guardianship until you reach your majority." The earl hesitated. "George had nothing good to say about her; I wish for you to be prepared so that you will not react when the solicitor reads the will." When he saw Darcy nod, he continued. "When you turn one and twenty, guardianship reverts to you and Richard." He shrugged. "I do not know why, but nothing my brother did ever made sense to anyone but him."

"She will be happy to hear this news." Elizabeth's whispered words led to murmured acknowledgements from the others.

Darcy looked to his uncle again. "Is there anything else?"

Matlock shook his head. "Nothing significant."

Darcy stood. "Then, I should like to retire and consider everything you have said."

The earl nodded as he rose. "That is an excellent idea." He held his hand out to the countess. "We will follow suit, if your aunt agrees."

Lady Matlock nodded. "I do." She took her husband's arm after kissing Darcy and Elizabeth. "We will see you in the morning."

~~~***~~~

Three days later, George Darcy's solicitor arrived from London. The Darcys and Matlocks welcomed him with grace, giving him the best guest room Pemberley had to offer.

Lord Matlock informed the attorney of the plans that had been made. "We shall listen to the reading of the will on the morrow. I have told the estate's steward, Mr. John Wickham, that his presence is required. I assume you informed Mr. George Wickham that he was needed here, as well?"

"I did, your lordship. I sent a missive to the address on file, and sent a man to locate him with a second one, just in case." Mr. Isaac Sweete spoke imperiously, as though his importance was equal to that of a peer of the realm.

"Very good." Matlock waved a hand in the direction of the housekeeper. "Reynolds will show you to your room. We keep country hours
~~~

here; dinner is served at six sharp." With a nod, Matlock dismissed Sweete, turning on his heel and striding away, his wife, nephew, and niece following.

Mr. Sweete bowed, his teeth grinding. With a scowl, he turned to the housekeeper. "My chambers, if you please."

Mrs. Reynolds managed to maintain an impassive expression. She curtseyed and gestured to the stairs, indicating the man should precede her. In silence, she led him to his assigned room, only giving him her well-practiced speech about where the bell pull was located and how to obtain anything he needed or wanted once they arrived.

Later, during the evening meal, Darcy, Elizabeth, and their guests were making polite small talk when the doorbell rang, an unusual occurrence for so late in the day. Though Darcy and Lady Matlock both remarked on it, their conversation continued until Mrs. Reynolds appeared in the doorway with a haggard-looking John Wickham behind her.

"Sir -" The housekeeper's words were interrupted when Wickham stepped out from behind her.

"I apologize for interrupting you all. You, as well, Mrs. Reynolds." Wickham threw the housekeeper a beseeching look. When she curtseyed and exited the room, he turned back to the table.

"What has happened?" Lord Matlock rose, as did Darcy and the solicitor. "It is unlike you to be so agitated, in my experience."

Wickham bowed. "Yes, your lordship. Again, I apologize, but I have news and it …" he trailed off, choking up and visibly fighting tears. He took a deep breath and wiped his cheek on his shoulder. "It is about my son." He bowed his head. "I did my best to train him up the way he should go, but his mother was so concerned with money and status. When he caught Mr. George Darcy's attention, she encouraged it. I was worried what would happen." He turned red and looked at Darcy. "I apologize, Mr. Darcy."

Darcy shook his head. "There is no need. I know what manner of man my father was. Please continue. What has happened to George?"

"A couple years back, there were accusations made against my son. He was here for the summer. You were, as I understood it, spending that time with a friend." Wickham swallowed again. "George was accused of seducing the baker's daughter. When I asked him about it, he laughingly admitted it. I tried to make him marry the girl, but the master took his side and brushed it off. The girl was sent away, and, I was told, died in childbirth a few months later. Her brothers vowed revenge."

The five at the table looked at each other with wide eyes.

Wickham opened his mouth to speak again, choked up, and swallowed. "I do not know if George was unaware of the threats or if he thought the other men would have forgotten by now." He shook his head. "Regardless, when my son stepped off the stage, he was recognized. He -, I -" He swallowed. "George is dead. His body was delivered to my house a short while ago. He has been beaten to death."

Elizabeth and her aunt gasped, their hands flying up to cover their mouths. Darcy, who along with his uncle had remained standing while the steward spoke, dropped into his chair, his eyes wide.

Lord Matlock was the only one with the fortitude at that moment to speak. "I am sorry for your loss." He hesitated. "You are certain it was your son?"

"Yes." Wickham nodded. "His features were battered but recognizable. His skull was broken; this is the blow that killed him, I have no doubt." He paused, turning his hat once in his hands before resuming the tight grip he had had on it before. "I thought it was important for you to know."

"Thank you." Darcy, having come to grips with the news, rose. "My father would have wanted your son treated well, even in death. I would like to pay for his funeral, if you will allow it."

Wickham nodded his assent. "I will. Thank you. You are very kind. I am aware of how my son treated you. I apologize for that."

Darcy shook his head. "It was not your fault." He fell silent, not knowing what else to say.

Shortly thereafter, John Wickham turned to go, leaving the occupants of Pemberley to finish their meal.

Silence reigned in the dining room for a long time. Eventually, the earl cleared his throat. "This changes everything in regards to the will, I believe." He turned to Mr. Sweete. "Does it not? Now, even should Mrs. Darcy not fall with child, there is no George Wickham for Pemberley to be granted to."

The solicitor sniffed, lifting his chin. "No, there is not, but the final dispensation will, of course, be up to the discretion of the probate court. While it is likely that Mr. Darcy will inherit all, there is no way to guarantee it."

No one had anything to say after that, and once the meal was complete and the traditional separation of the sexes performed, it was unanimously decided that the party would retire for the night.

~~~***~~~

The reading of the will the next day went as expected, though Pemberley's steward did not attend. Nothing contained in the document was a surprise, and immediately following his explanation of it, the solicitor returned to London.

"Now, we wait." Darcy put his hands behind his back as he watched the carriage carrying Mr. Sweete drive away.

Lord Matlock clapped him on the shoulder. "Yes, we wait, but without George Wickham in the picture, I do not foresee anything but a victory for you."

"I hope so." Darcy sighed and turned to go into the house. "Elizabeth asked about my father's things." He glanced at his uncle. "I have no desire to go through them all at present."

"I should imagine not." The earl was quiet for a moment. "Your aunt and I have decided to remain here at Pemberley for the immediate future. I suggest you allow me to go through any papers your father left. His clothing and other personal effects can be boxed up and moved to the attics until such time as you desire to deal
~~~

with them." He tilted his head to look at Darcy as they strode through the hall. "Are you considering moving into his rooms?"

Darcy pressed his lips together. "Yes, I am. I would like to redecorate first, though, and to do that, Father's things must be removed." He started up the steps.

"That is an excellent notion." The earl was silent until they arrived at the top of the staircase, at which time he stopped, his nephew stopping with him. "I want you to know that I consider this your estate. I will help you learn whatever you need to, and I will assist you in reviewing the ledgers, but this is your home. If you want to redecorate or anything else, you are free to. You do not require my permission."

Darcy lifted his lips in a small smile. "Thank you, Uncle."

~~~***~~~

The next three months passed quickly, with Darcy throwing himself into learning the ins and outs of the estate and Elizabeth immersing herself into the running of the house. Before long, the baby made its presence known in more than just morning sickness and exhaustion. The young couple rejoiced. Even sweeter was the fact that the quickening came on Darcy's birthday.
~~~

On the appointed day, the earl and countess, along with Darcy, Georgiana, and a visibly-pregnant Elizabeth appeared in front of the church's probate court. This appearance had required a trip to London. The court, with proof before them that Darcy had met the requirements, immediately handed control of Pemberley and Georgiana over to him. The family celebrated with a private dinner at Matlock House, where they had decided to stay.

Two days later, the Darcys made the return trip to Pemberley. Elizabeth was insistent on giving birth at home, and so was willing to go through the discomfort of the rough roads for four days.

Epilogue

When they arrived, Georgiana was there to greet them, alongside her governess. Miss Robinson smirked at Darcy and Elizabeth, her insolence not going unnoticed by either of them. With his sister on one arm and his wife on the other, Darcy escorted the ladies inside, the governess trailing behind. He leaned toward Elizabeth to whisper to her.

"Today is as good a day as any to get rid of an employee, is it not?" When Elizabeth looked up at him, Darcy tipped his head back.

With a quick glance over her shoulder, Elizabeth nodded. "Indeed it is, Master of Pemberley."

Darcy winked as he let go of his ladies. He handed his hat, coat, and gloves to the waiting maid before speaking. "Georgiana, I am eager to hear all about how you have spent the last couple of weeks, but I need to speak to Miss Robinson first. Please go to the family parlor with Elizabeth and wait for me. I will join you shortly."

"I will, but hurry. I have missed you!" Georgiana hugged her brother quickly, then took her sister's hand and went with her down the hall to the aforementioned room, chattering all the way.

Darcy turned toward the governess, ignoring for the time being the sneer on the woman's face. "Please come into the study." He turned on his heel and made his way into what had once been his father's domain. He strode around the desk, seating himself behind it. He leaned his arms against the edge of the desktop, linking his fingers together. He did not invite the woman to sit, nor did he look at her for a long moment. When he had his thoughts gathered together, he lifted his eyes, catching the speculative look in hers as she allowed them to wander down what she could see of his form. *I shall have to bathe after this*, he thought.

"Miss Robinson, there has been no love lost between us. For whatever reason, my father kept you on, despite your lack of attention to your charge. Mr. George Darcy is, as you know, now dead, and I have been granted the rights to Pemberley as part of my inheritance. I am now terminating your employment, effective immediately. You will pack your bags and depart within the hour."

Shock suffused Miss Robinson's face, followed swiftly by a scowl. "You cannot fire me. Who will teach your precious sister? Your wife?" As she always did when referencing Elizabeth, the governess sneered that last word.

Instantly, Darcy was on his feet, his countenance darkened and his eyes narrowed to slits. "Yes, my wife. You will not refer to her in such a rude manner, and I *can* fire you. If you do not leave my presence this instant and if you are not out of this house in one hour, you will not receive a reference. The choice is yours."

"Your father promised me a permanent position and a place in your bed." Her scowl disappeared as Miss Robinson again drew her eyes down Darcy's body. "With that chit indisposed, you will need someone to warm you at night." Her eyes drew upwards to stare at Darcy. "A man like you has needs. I know this."

Disgusted at her first words, Darcy stepped backwards, the backs of his legs hitting the chair. It was his turn to sneer. "I am not my father, and it was not his place to make you promises of that kind. He is dead and buried and any pledges of that sort that he made are null and void. You are to leave Pemberley this instant. I will have Mrs. Reynolds send your things on." He reached behind him and pulled the bell as the governess began to scream at him.

The housekeeper appeared within seconds, two footmen behind her. She took in the scene and said something to the servants, who immediately took hold of Miss Robinson and began to move her toward the door.

"I am sorry, sir." Mrs. Reynolds waited for Darcy to give her instructions.

Taking a deep breath, Darcy relaxed as the governess was removed from his study. Looking at the housekeeper, he informed her of his decision. "I was going to give her an hour to collect her belongings, but changed my mind. I want her out of here, removed from Pemberley property, at once. You may pack her bags and send them on to her. I am letting her go without a reference."

Mrs. Reynolds did nothing but nod and curtsey before leaving, but Darcy could swear he saw the ghost of a smile on the housekeeper's face. He wondered what the woman knew that he did not, but decided it did not matter.

~~~***~~~

Elizabeth heartily approved of Darcy's decision regarding Miss Robinson. With the assistance of Lady Matlock and Mrs. Reynolds, a search was begun for a replacement. In the meantime, Elizabeth took charge of her sister's education, an action that ended up drawing the two closer together.

Georgiana took her sister as a model, and as the years passed and she grew to adulthood,
~~~

would adopt many of Elizabeth's mannerisms and tendencies, making her a lively, happy, and discerning young woman.

As Elizabeth had said to Lady Matlock on the wild ride home to Pemberley when George Darcy died, Elizabeth found she had to daily forgive her parents, aunt, and uncle for forcing her to marry against her will. She maintained an active correspondence with her sisters, especially with Jane.

Darcy also struggled with forgiveness. In his case, it was more difficult, in large part because he had no understanding of his father's reasons for being so harsh. Letters between himself and the earl were frequent, and Darcy came to treasure his mother's brother, and to see him as a father figure. It was, however, Elizabeth who helped him the most by reminding him that he was already a better man than his father had been, and by reiterating her belief that he would be an excellent father.

~~~***~~~

On a cold day in January, Elizabeth delivered her baby, a healthy boy with a lusty cry. Darcy held them both that night and sobbed with relief that God had spared their lives. They decided to name the child Henry Charles Andrew
~~~

Darcy. Elizabeth affectionately referred to him as "Harry," which made Darcy cringe.

When the time came to name Harry's god-parents, Darcy asked the earl and countess, and his friend, Charles Bingley. After the christening ceremony, when the family had returned, Bingley cornered him.

"My father has leased an estate for the next year. Perhaps you and Mrs. Darcy can bring your sister and little Harry and spend the summer with us."

Darcy tilted his head. "Perhaps we could. Where is this estate located?"

"It is in Hertfordshire, near a town named Meryton." Bingley jumped when Darcy choked on his port. "I say man, are you well?"

"I am well, only surprised," Darcy said when he could speak again. What is the name of the estate?"

"Netherfield. We move in next month." Bingley's brow contained an unusual-for-him furrow. "Are you certain you are well?"

"Yes, I am." Darcy paused. "I was surprised because Elizabeth's father's estate is near Meryton."

"I see." Bingley followed his friend's gaze to where Mrs. Darcy was seated. "How does the wind blow on that front?"

Darcy shrugged. "Well, I think. In some ways, she has more to overcome. She was her father's favorite until her seventeenth birthday. I never had my father's affection."

Bingley had nothing to say to that, and so remained silent.

~~~***~~~

The Darcys did spend that summer with the Bingleys. Caroline, about to turn eighteen and preparing for her first season, found it difficult to be polite to Elizabeth, who had been the cause of all her hopes and desires being crushed. However, her parents were sharp eyed and alert to any mis-steps their children might make that had the potential to keeping them out of the higher circles of society. They immediately recognized their youngest daughter's jealousy and dealt with it swiftly and effectively.

Once it was decided that she and her family would travel to Hertfordshire, Elizabeth chose to speak to her parents once and for all. She had received one letter from them in the year of her marriage, and that was from her mother, with all manner of instruction on how to keep a home and her husband's attention, and included a single line from her father. She asked Darcy to
~~~

accompany her to Longbourn, to which he agreed.

Arriving at the house she had not seen since she left for her wedding trip, Elizabeth was engulfed in the sounds and smells of the place. Mrs. Hill had hugged her tightly and welcomed her back, then led the pair to Mr. Bennet's book room. The conversation inside was tense, especially at first, but Elizabeth and Darcy had agreed to simply express their forgiveness and let anything else go. They were therefore able, when Mr. Bennet refused to acknowledge anything about his actions being wrong or reprehensible, to smile and bid him a good day. They retired to the drawing room and spent a large part of the morning visiting with Mrs. Bennet and her daughters.

From that day, though her relationship with her parents was never what it had been before, Elizabeth was able to greet them with equanimity at dinners and balls. She was delighted to watch Jane fall in love with Bingley, and stood up with her sister when she married him.

For Darcy, the road to forgiveness and peace took a far longer time. There were moments as his children aged that he feared he was turning into his father, for the four boys and both girls tried his patience, seemingly on purpose.

His wife, however, insisted that he was nothing like his father and took time to point out the myriad of things Darcy did that his father had not. Eventually, he came to accept that being a better man did not involve being perfect. After that, he was better able to enjoy his children and grandchildren. Whenever he was asked the secret to his happy marriage and family, he would point to Elizabeth and say, "My unwanted bride turned out to be the best thing that happened to me."

The End

Before you go …

If you enjoyed this book, please consider leaving a review at the store where you purchased it.

Also, consider joining my mailing list at https://mailchi.mp/ee42ccbc6409/zoeburton signup

~Zoe

About the Author

Zoe Burton first fell in love with Jane Austen's books in 2010, after seeing the 2005 version of Pride and Prejudice on television. While making her purchases of Miss Austen's novels, she discovered Jane Austen Fan Fiction; soon after that she found websites full of JAFF. Her life has never been the same. She began writing her own stories when she ran out of new ones to read.

Zoe lives in a 100-plus-year-old house in the snow-belt of Ohio with her Boxer, Jasper. She is a former Special Education Teacher, and has a passion for romance in general, *Pride and Prejudice* in particular, and stock car racing.

Connect with Zoe Burton

Email:
zoe@zoeburton.com

Facebook:
https://www.facebook.com/ZoeBurtonBooks

https://www.facebook.com/groups/Burtons Babes/

Pinterest:
https://www.pinterest.com/zoeburtonauthor/

Instagram:
https://www.instagram.com/zoeburtonauthor/

Website:
https://zoeburton.com

Join my mailing list:
https://mailchi.mp/ee42ccbc6409/zoeburton signup

Support me at Patreon:
https://www.patreon.com/zoeburtonauthor

Me at Austen Authors:
http://austenauthors.net/zoe-burton/

More by Zoe Burton

Regency Single Titles:

I Promise To…

Lilacs & Lavender

Promises Kept

Bits of Ribbon and Lace

Decisions and Consequences

Mr. Darcy's Love

Darcy's Deal

The Essence of Love

Matches Made at Netherfield

Darcy's Perfect Present

Darcy's Surprise Betrothal

To Save Elizabeth

Darcy Overhears

Merry Christmas, Mr. Darcy!

Darcy's Secret Marriage

Darcy's Christmas Compromise

Darcy's Predicament

Darcy's Uneasy Betrothal

Darcy's Yuletide Wedding

Victorian Romance:

A MUCH Later Meeting

Westerns:

Darcy's Bodie Mine

Bundles:

Darcy's Adventures

Forced to Wed

Promises

Mr. Darcy Finds Love (available exclusively to newsletter subscribers)

The Darcy Marriage Series Books 1-3

Mr. Darcy, My Hero

Coming Together

Christmas in Meryton

The Darcy Marriage Series:

Darcy's Wife Search

Lady Catherine Impedes

Caroline's Censure

Pride & Prejudice & Racecars

Darcy's Race to Love

Georgie's Redemption

Darcy's Caution